HAUNTING ON SEAFOAM STREET

A Cinnamon Bay Romance

BREA VIRAGH

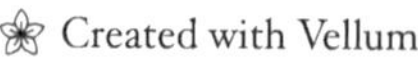 Created with Vellum

The possibility of a future romance is threatened by past mistakes that won't die.

Associate Camp Director Spring Astin knows what she wants from a relationship, and Cinnamon Bay newcomer Marshall Rownan is just the man to deliver. Unfortunately, he isn't biting.

Their shared love of the paranormal brings them to the investigation of one of the Bay's most haunted homes, but the only ghosts they can find are those of relationships past. Spring knows her heart and mind better than most and is ready to hand over both to Marshall within moments of meeting him.

Reeling from all the mistakes he's made and forced to take leave from his teaching position, Marshall wants to focus on the haunting. He has no time for someone like Spring when his life has been nothing but a series of bad things happening to him.

Fans of Brenda Novak and Robyn Carr will fall in love with this brand new shared world that combines romance, mystery, and magic in the quirky coastal town of Cinnamon Bay, North Carolina.

CHAPTER ONE

Skeletons danced in the wickedly warm wind brought in by the sea. It caused candle flames inside jack-o-lanterns to flicker and held hints of salt and autumn within it.

It was that time of year again. The most wonderful time of year, according to Spring Astin.

Halloween.

It was a time to indulge her inner fantasies. Not the ordinary fantasies, the ones better left in a darkened room with silken sheets and maybe wine and roses. Those kinds of fantasies she possessed in abundance, if she were being one hundred percent honest.

No, these were her other fantasies. The ones she'd entertained as a child and got to act out for a full twenty-four hours. One day out of three hundred and sixty-four others. Thoughts of dressing up as a pirate or princess, a cat or a clown. Thoughts of embracing magic and using a spell to call down the moon.

Spring got into Halloween like some people celebrated Christmas. She decked out her beach house with strings of orange and black lights. There were three or four pumpkins on the stoop and another couple on the steps leading up, as well as gourds and squash galore. There were witches on the lawn and ghouls hanging from the palm trees.

Not to mention she'd visited every haunted house within a hundred miles. Whenever she could, and wherever she traveled, she went on the local ghost tours. It was her secret passion. The one that only her closest friends knew about because, really, people would think her nuts if they found out how much anything paranormal fascinated her.

It was easier to say she was nuts about Halloween. She had a difficult time finding people who shared her love of the supernatural. Most of the time she stuck to safe topics of conversation, like candy.

Everyone loved candy.

The neighborhood trick-or-treaters knew *she* had the best candy, too. She didn't go for the little mini pieces. She sprang for king-sized bars. The good stuff. The kind that made even the grumpiest child happier than they'd been before arriving at her house.

The rest of the town only knew of her enthusiasm for Halloween, when she gave herself permission to go all out. Luckily, most of the other denizens of Cinnamon Bay did the same, so she wasn't alone.

"This is going to be so much fun," she muttered with a giggle.

A sudden flashlight beam across her face robbed her of vision momentarily and Spring hissed, slapping it away from her.

"Get that thing out of my face! Are you trying to blind me? Watch where you point the light."

"I'm sorry!" Her best friend, Mecca, sounded anything but. In fact, if Spring had to hazard a guess, and if the chattering teeth were any indication... "I'm t-terrified."

"Why are you terrified?" Spring wanted to know.

"Because I've never been in a real haunted house before

and I feel like we're trespassing. We *are* trespassing, aren't we? Oh, I never should have let you talk me into this."

Spring sighed, willing her vision to return on the double so she could see more than spots and shadows. She pushed her long ponytail over her shoulder. "It's not trespassing. Braving the house on Seafoam Street is like a rite of passage. Every year, kids dare each other to spend an entire night in the house. This is your time, girl. It's practically tradition. And tonight is your initiation. Now you're one of the cool kids."

An answering huff, almost a whine. "I don't want it to be my time. I never wanted to be one of the cool kids."

The tiny coastal hamlet of Cinnamon Bay, North Carolina, had their own claim to fame in the haunting department. Not just a house. An entire street. Seafoam Street was on the outskirts of town in the old historic section, and although most of the buildings had since been condemned, one stood firm in the face of weather and adversity.

Seafoam House.

The matron of the block, the jewel of the street's crown, the—

Spring could practically hear the other woman's knees clacking. "It's fine, Mecca, jeez!" she insisted. "A ghost is not going to jump out and eat you. And the police aren't going to arrest you, either. Calm down."

"We had to squeeze through a chain on the fence, Spring! And then squeeze through an unlocked window? That's not normal!" Mecca heard the scrabbling of little claws on the old wood floor and screeched, whirling around, her sneakers skidding through dirt and grime. "What the hell?"

"It's just rats. Probably."

"Ugh! Rats are disgusting."

"But not as scary as ghosts." Spring was trying to reassure her friend but knew she came up short when Mecca groaned.

"I can't believe I let you talk me into this," Mecca

repeated. In the dim reflected light of the flashlights they each held, she saw dirt spots on the knees of her skinny jeans and a spider web draped across her left shoulder. She batted at the web frantically. "Eww!"

Spring couldn't hold back a grin. She'd been in the house many times before, the first time on a dare between her and two other friends, neither of whom still kept in touch. Most of her memory of that night was a huge blank spot accompanied by a cold chill down her back.

Which led Spring to believe she'd been an honest to goodness witness to the paranormal. Her very first ghost encounter! And she'd been hooked ever since.

She loved the thrill of it, the uncertainty of the tantalizing unknown, the possibility that there was more than human eyes could see, a whole universe more in fact. It sent shivers along her spine. Wow, she was such an adventure seeker.

And yes, technically it *was* trespassing to be inside the house. But the town turned a blind eye as long as no one was hurt and there was no vandalism.

It had been time to get Mecca in on the experience, something they could share and discuss together. Sadly, her best friend wasn't having it. She found it terrifying when someone jumped around a corner yelling *boo*.

The flashlight was back in her face and Spring hissed, taking a swipe at it and missing.

"We need to go upstairs. There's a cold spot in the upper bedroom that no one has been able to explain," Spring stated. "Plus cameras have caught shifting shadows and orbs floating in midair."

"I don't care. I don't like this," Mecca said, shifting away from the staircase when Spring marched toward the steps.

"You don't have to like it. It's not like we're trying to *catch* a ghost, here. We just want to have a little fun!" A smile spread over her face and it took everything inside of Spring not to rub her hands together and laugh maniacally.

"Fun! This is supposed to be *fun?*" Mecca shivered. "Do you really think this place is haunted?"

"I absolutely do!" She'd witnessed it firsthand, hadn't she? Wood creaked as she hauled herself to the next step. Then the next. "Use this time to get out of your own head. You're too uptight. You need to embrace the visceral reaction of your fear. It will do you good."

Mecca stared up at her and grimaced. "That sounds demented."

"It's good for you," Spring insisted. Then swatted nervously above her head when something invisible brushed against her.

"You're insane. You know that, right?"

"Yep!"

They made their way up the stairs of the quaint old Victorian, each step creaking beneath their weight. There was a threadbare runner tacked on the stairs with little golden nails, now dulled. It was the only hint left of the house's former grandeur.

Houses had a personality peculiar to each. This one, if she could have described it in any way, would be a hungry old woman. Much like the Hens, the three matchmakers who had taken up residence in the boardwalk coffee shop, Spring thought with a smile.

Yes, this place definitely reminded her of Hattie, Trixie, and Birdie. Waiting for a fresh mark and ready to pounce. How Spring had managed to stay one step ahead of their matchmaking attempts these past few years she would never know.

"I don't like this," Mecca said again with a low groan.

Spring kept her voice soft, as though the walls were listening, overhearing every word. "It's exciting, isn't it?"

An aging floorboard groaned and creaked somewhere inside. Somewhere other than the staircase they were ascending. Spring stilled at the top of the stairs, her gaze drifting left and then right as she swung her flashlight.

Were they the only ones in the house?

She didn't want to give in to the niggling sensation beneath her collar bone telling her to panic and run. But it was hard to resist, with the hour approaching midnight, and branches from the palm trees outside scratching at the windows and walls like fingernails. The brisk sea wind rattled doors and glass.

"Spring?" Mecca whispered, shifting closer to Spring until they touched.

"It's nothing," she whispered back. And part of her hoped it was so, while another part still fervently wished for unexplained chills and thrills.

Until she caught a glimpse of a distorted shadow slipping across the upper hallway ceiling. Riveted, she tracked it with her eyes, body frozen, her breathing slow but her heart racing. Sweat made her palms slick and threatened her hold on the flashlight.

"What did you say happened to the people who used to live here?" Mecca asked in a tinny voice.

Spring took another moment to stare at the point where she'd seen—or thought she'd seen—the moving shadow. But nothing else happened, and apparently Mecca hadn't seen it at all.

"Oh, they were murdered." Her friend's *eep* brought her to laughter. "I'm kidding! The house was built about a hundred and fifty years ago. The story goes that the wood used to build it came from a ship that wrecked in Cinnamon Bay during a bad storm. So right there you've got the makings of sailor ghosts attached to the very wood as a result of sudden and violent death. Then the property bounced around from family member to family member because no one would live in it for very long. Legend tells of ghost sightings of a tall man and a little girl, although it's not clear whether they were part of the original family or not. I think there might have been a lot of people who died here over the years. Anyway, it was sold and resold until eventually no one wanted it at all and the place went up for auction. The town bought it for historical purposes, but it's been empty for decades because there was no money available for preservation. But that doesn't stop people from wanting to get inside for a glimpse of a ghost. Especially at Halloween. *Woo-ooo-oooooo!*"

"Stop that! You know what? I don't want to do this anymore. I have a man waiting for me at home with a seafood boil and it's getting late."

"Carter cooked you a seafood boil? At midnight?"

Mecca trembled. "I'm lying. I just want to go home."

Another floorboard creaked somewhere and Mecca lurched forward, pushing Spring farther onto the landing. The two women clasped hands.

"Has anyone ever done a séance here?" Mecca continued.

"I think a few people have, but it's never been televised. If it were, I believe Seafoam House would be right up there with the rest of the bigwig hauntings in the country. Like Amityville in New York."

Mecca didn't like that idea, if her tightening fingers were any indication.

They shuffled slowly down the hallway and passed under a curtain of cold air like sheets of ribbon in the wind.

"Did you feel that?"

Spring nodded emphatically. "I sure did!"

A dried palm frond crashed against a downstairs window and Mecca screamed. The resounding boom had Spring's heart rushing to her throat. Mecca grabbed her other hand and pulled her down the staircase.

"That's it, I'm out of here!" Mecca wasted no time in bolting toward the kitchen and the window Spring had shoved her through earlier.

"Aw, come on, I'm sure it's nothing bad!" Still, Spring

glanced over her shoulder at what sounded like laughter coming from behind her.

"Doesn't matter, I'm out. Have a wonderful night, girl, but I am done. Never coming back. Finished. *Finito*."

Mecca howled when Spring grabbed hold of her pants and tried to drag her back. "Don't leave me alone in here!"

In the end, she scrambled outside on the heels of her best friend, knowing in time they'd look back on tonight and laugh, but finding no humor at the moment in the delicious chills skittering through her.

CHAPTER TWO

"You're going to love it here," Uncle Jack told him with a wry grin. "By the end of your vacation, you're going to be begging me not to drive you to the airport. Trust me. I know what I'm talking about."

The sleeves of his garish red-and-white Hawaiian shirt were pushed up toward his biceps, revealing a wrinkled and faded tattoo of a bare-breasted mermaid on his right arm.

Marshall Rownan grimaced, the sun glaring down in an attempt to blind him. Was it brighter here? Or had he spent too much of his time stuck inside a classroom to appreciate the weather in this part of the South?

Vacation, Jack said. *That* was a word that stuck in his craw.

Marshall hadn't wanted to take a break in the middle of the semester. He hadn't wanted a break ever, really, because he loved his work. He adored what he did and the direction he'd chosen for his life, choosing to throw himself into classes and lab.

Unfortunately, his superiors thought it was a good idea, what with his recent episodes. Thus why he'd had to endure a plane ride from hell sitting next to a toddler who liked to throw pudding.

He flicked at a piece of dried chocolate on his shirt collar and continued to stare out the window. "I'm only here for a couple of weeks until Halloween, Uncle Jack. And then I'm going right back to New York where I belong. There's no convincing me otherwise."

He couldn't be away from the department any longer than that. Despite their urging him to enjoy himself.

He'd agreed to a mental health break. Fourteen days. Nothing more.

It wasn't like he wanted to be in North Carolina, in the middle of nowhere. Not when he had important research waiting for his attention back home.

"I don't know why you lugged your equipment down here. For two weeks?" Jack blew a raspberry and pulled the old pickup truck off the highway. "You had to pay extra for your junk to be shipped to the house. Just to turn right around and ship it back?"

"Let me worry about the money," Marshall argued. Seafoam Street was the only silver lining to this forced vacation, and one he planned to make the most of. He'd get to investigate the alleged haunting of Seafoam House before anyone knew where he'd gone.

Around them, the scenery changed. The landscape opened and if he stared long enough Marshall could almost imagine he saw the ocean through the trees.

"Seems like a waste," Jack continued gruffly. "Doesn't matter, though. I'm gonna sell you on this place." He reached out and punched his nephew good-naturedly on the arm. "You mark my words, Marshie boy."

He resisted the urge to rub his arm. Also resisted the urge to remind his favorite uncle that he hated the nickname "Marshie". Luckily only Uncle Jack called him that. "I think I would miss the changing seasons too much."

"We have seasons here. Hot and *hotter*. There you go. Take your pick. You don't need seasons to capture ghosts."

Marshall's chuckle died in his throat. All that time and energy spent on an electrical engineering degree, followed by a coveted professorship at NYU, and this was what his family knew about him? That he captured ghosts?

"Is that what you think I do? Trap them in a little box?" he couldn't help but ask. Like he was a regular *Ghostbuster* because of his hobby. Maybe he should invest in a jumpsuit with the popular logo on the front pocket.

"You should be on one of those television shows," Jack said, pointing one stubby finger toward the windshield for emphasis.

Marshall sighed, lips twitching. The weight of this trip pressed down on him at once, along with a good bit of heat despite it being October. In New York, the weather had begun to cool, the trees taking on the crisp oranges and reds of the season. Here in Cinnamon Bay, those kinds of changes didn't exist. Or if they did, they came much later.

"I'm not really interested in being in front of a camera. Publishing, yes." He fingered the camera on his lap. "I'm hoping this investigation will be different from the last one." He hadn't been able to find a winner since his last bungled project.

It was his attitude, he knew. A self-proclaimed curmudgeon, he would rather be in an archive surrounded by research materials or in his study tinkering on his latest gizmo than standing in front of a camera. Which meant his version of fame came with a leather spine namesake instead of a shiny TV contract.

"What do you mean? Different how?" Jack pushed.

"Investigating paranormal phenomena documented over three decades, in a place where people don't shy away...they embrace the crazy. The abnormal. I haven't seen anything like it."

Marshall spoke, of course, of Seafoam Street. The hauntings centered on one house at the end of the block, but the community had taken the sightings and run with them. Now the whole street garnered attention and the houses there—even the rundown derelict ones—were worth more than the houses of the neighboring streets.

He'd never seen such a crazy thing.

Investigating the *beyond* was something Marshall had started in his spare time to impress an ex-girlfriend, one who'd taken the haunted Freedom Trail tour one too many times and convinced herself it was her destiny to expose the paranormal to the public eye. Hannah was something else, especially when she got herself wrapped up in an idea.

Admittedly, he was skeptical at first. He was one of those people who kept his feet firmly planted on the ground so that his head didn't swirl off into the clouds. But he'd been caught up in it nevertheless. He enjoyed the mystery, the aura of the unknown and unexplainable that came with alleged hauntings. He'd never *seen* anything, of course.

But that didn't keep him from trying. Now he did it because he loved it. The scientist in him still had an urge to debunk, but secretly he craved indisputable validation that there really *are* more things in heaven and earth, Horatio.

"I'm sure there are other places, kiddo. I invited you down here to enjoy yourself for once," Jack continued, speaking as though he knew what was best. "To get out of that little closet you call an office. Feel some sunshine on your skin and salt breeze in your hair."

"I feel plenty of sun on my skin," Marshall grumbled.

"You're gonna burn to a crisp with that glue-tone you call a tan. Get out while you're here, kid, I'm begging of you, and maybe meet a girl."

Caterpillar eyebrows waggled with the sentiment.

Yeah, this again. Marshall had heard enough of it from his parents. Thirty years old and still not married. He needed to catch up with his peers and settle down. Blah, blah. Then once his father decided he'd be better off with a new younger girlfriend rather than his longtime wife, Marshall had heard it from his mother alone.

"What are you, the town matchmaker?"

"Ha!" Jack let out a seal-bark laugh. "I'm a fisherman. I spend my life on the sea. It leaves little time for matchmaking. I hardly get to see the kids I have. Scattered to the four winds, they are."

And with different mothers. "But you make time for your favorite nephew."

"Sounds about right."

It had been years since Marshall had seen his uncle, which was why it surprised him when the offer came. They weren't exactly the closest family. Raised by a single mother in the Northeast once dear old Dad packed it in, he'd spent most of his teenage and adult life with his nose buried in a book rather than enjoying any so-called family time. When Emmie Rownan decided she wanted to move down to God-knew-where North Carolina to be closer to her brother two years ago, Marshall hadn't objected.

He also hadn't followed.

He didn't consider himself a big nature buff, or a water enthusiast, so living close to the ocean was not a draw. He spent most of his time in either his office or a classroom, with his glasses on and his attention in a thousand places at once.

Marshall believed he was slowly going out of his mind—in the best way. And apparently, the rest of his coworkers thought the same. Lose it on one freshman who refuses to turn in their homework and you get labeled a basket case for eternity.

Emotional upheaval could push even the sanest man toward a breakdown. Toxic relationships did that to a person.

There was a slight bump as Jack drove over a pothole.

When Marshall looked out the window again, he saw they were approaching the town.

He took in the rows of vibrantly painted beach houses, palm trees spearing up toward the blue sky, and the quiet streets with rows of cars parked in front of businesses.

"Storybook quaint," he said under his breath.

"What was that?" Jack asked, his arm scooping the air out the open window so that the salty breeze ruffled his hair. "I didn't hear you."

"Nothing."

They drove through town and passed a bank, post office, market. A few places to eat. The streets were leading, he could see now, to a very busy boardwalk with ample parking. Or it might have been ample parking in the off season, but he had a feeling that in the summer it would be difficult to find a parking space.

Luckily his *mental health break* had coincided with the approaching autumn. Bad for the middle of the semester and the work he still needed to accomplish. Good for his forced vacation to Cinnamon Bay. At least now he wouldn't have to deal with sweltering hotter-than-hell temperatures. Loads of tourists still, because a picturesque coastal town like this would attract visitors year-round, but those he could avoid if he stayed away from the busier, trendier spots.

Ah, *there* was the beach.

"Put those glasses away, kid, and take out your shades," Jack advised. He shot his nephew a glance that spoke volumes.

"These are transitional. They're as dark as they can get."

"And they aren't dark enough to keep you from going blind. Once that sun hits the sand you are going to be in for a world of trouble. Trust me." Jack pointed to his own wrinkles. Crow's feet? More like ostrich feet. "I know a thing or two."

They found a parking spot without any trouble, and at once Marshall felt his stomach rolling over when he saw the crowds still crisscrossing beach and boardwalk. There were so many people around, the holidays ahead and the lure of continued nice weather drawing in tourists and vacationers alike despite it being October already.

He was supposed to be doing the same—taking some time off to get his head on straight. Taking it easy. Pretending to be a tourist or vacationer. Neither of which he'd ever felt comfortable with.

All he could think about was work. How much he missed his office and his neat little apartment in the city. The way he crawled home after a busy but satisfying day and buried himself in his sanctuary.

But he allowed Jack to lead him along the boardwalk and take in the sights. There was a bookstore he immediately wanted to investigate and was promptly pulled away from without argument.

He had to admit he liked the look of the place. Sure, it was busy, with children and adults pushing their way along the weathered wooden boards, in and out of shops. The display windows were cheerful and designed to draw in business. The graying clapboard exteriors of the stores were dressed up with lively colors through shutters, planter boxes, flags, or patio furniture.

"We're making a pit stop before I drop you off at your haunted pile of rubbish, since I know that's where you want to head first," Jack said in a good-natured grumbling kind of way. His eyes were narrowed against the harsh rays of the sun, lines worn deep into his skin from too many years outside. "I need a fix."

"A fix of what?"

"You'll see."

Marshall glanced up at the coffee shop sign and banner flickering in the breeze—Brew with a View. His first thought was *wow*. He'd noticed the tantalizing aroma in the air but figured it was his intense desire for caffeine playing tricks on him.

He appreciated the shop even more once they stepped through the front doors. There was a large bar and checkout counter spanning the entire rear of the room. Copper steamers sat to the left, with a display cooler for desserts and sandwiches on the right. When he turned around, the entire front of the store was a row of windows looking out at the gas lamps lining the boardwalk. Beyond that was the ocean.

The owners definitely had a great view.

Tables and chairs were scattered across the room, all taken, and the only empty seats were beside a trio of older ladies who looked like they'd staked a claim at the bar. Marshall's first thought was to stay far, *far* away from them. Especially when they turned as a single unit to stare at him.

Through him.

"Come on." Jack beckoned him forward and they crossed the room, closer to the little gnome-like women sitting on high stools at the coffee bar. "Hattie, Trixie. *Birdie*." He sent a wink to the last one, although all three ladies tittered in appreciation.

"You old charmer," the closest one croaked, coyly adjusting her wide-brimmed hat. "What did you bring us today?"

They eyed Marshall up and down in unison. A practiced move, probably. He was fresh meat here, and he had enough of his brain left to recognize that.

"My nephew. Marshall Rownan, say hello to the belles of the Bay. These ladies haven't left their posts in this coffee shop since it opened."

Jack made the round of introductions and Marshall held out his hand to each. All three ladies had skin like dried paper. He was afraid to squeeze their hands too hard lest he snap a bone. "It's a pleasure to meet you all," Marshall stated with a smile. "My uncle has told me many wonderful things."

Not exactly a lie. Jack had had plenty to say about the Bay itself, but he'd never mentioned these women.

"And how long with your nephew be staying with us, Jackie Boy?" the last one asked on a sigh of sound.

Birdie, maybe? Marshall couldn't be sure. She had red-orange dyed hair properly primped under a jaunty beret and more rings on her fingers than a display at a jeweler's shop.

"Only a couple of weeks," Marshall answered for himself. He drove his hands into the pockets of his pants when he wasn't sure what to do with them. "Then it's back to work for me."

"And where is work, young man?"

"New York. I'm a professor at NYU."

Then when he sensed a lull in their attention, he quietly excused himself from the conversation and approached the counter.

An attractive brunette greeted him with a warm smile. She wiped her grounds-dusted palms on the front of her black apron. "What can I get for you, sweetheart?"

A little nonplussed by the unexpected endearment—that would *never* happen in New York City—Marshall squinted at the chalkboard menu. "I'm not sure," he replied.

"It can be a little overwhelming for newbies, I know," the brunette said with a smile. "Might I make a suggestion?"

The woman pointed behind her, finger landing on the option third from the bottom. "This is a special we're running for the warmer months, a cool twist on the specialty brew we're known for. It's been recently put back on the menu and more popular than ever."

"What specialty brew *are* you known for?" Marshall asked, not having heard anything about it before.

"It's a spice blend we combine with espresso and secrets. Some of the locals will even tell you that it helps you fall in love." The woman gave him a saucy wink. "If you believe in those sorts of superstitions."

Marshall worried the inside of his cheek, lips pursed. "I don't need or want any help with that, thanks." Not that he had anyone waiting at home. He just preferred to keep things simple. And right now, simple meant single.

"Ah, well, maybe an Americano. You've got the look of a serious coffee drinker."

"You're right on the Americano, and..." He paused, turning to glance at his uncle. "I'm not sure what Uncle Jack—"

"Oh, Jack always gets the same thing," she said and waved him off. "Black, straight up. He never deviates."

It sounded like Jack. Black, straight up. "One of your regulars, eh?"

"You know it. *Uncle* Jack...so you must be Marshall. We've heard a lot about you. I'm Eva Halloway. Shoot, no. Jenssen. Married name takes a bit of getting used to. Eva *Jenssen*," she clarified.

Great. Jack had been running his mouth. Marshall could only wince at what probably came out of it. "Well, nice to meet you, Eva," he said without a hint of a grimace, reaching out to shake her hand. He probably wouldn't remember the name, but he'd try. Especially if the coffee was as tasty as it smelled. He might brave the crowds for something *that* good.

Marshall patiently waited for the order to be filled, his Americano taking little time, and was surprised when Eva pushed a tiny cup of cool liquid his way while she worked. He brought it to his nose, inhaling deeply and catching whiffs of orange, cinnamon, and allspice.

"The trio loves to push it on everyone who walks through the door. So lately I've taken to beating them to the punch. They weren't happy with me for the first few days. It's a game we play," Eva told him over her shoulder. "There's nothing bad in there, I promise."

She must have seen the skepticism on his face. Unfortunately, he didn't want to tell her it was his natural expression.

A professor's version of "resting bitch face" and one he could not readily shake.

Marshall tossed back the sample in one swig, just to be polite. "It's good." Surprisingly delicious. And he'd never been one for sweet drinks.

"Better than good, but I'll take what I can get. That will be five-fifty," she said as she placed the large container of Americano in front of him along with a smaller cup for Jack.

"Cheap," he commented as he dug in his back pocket for his wallet.

"It's how we bring 'em back," Eva told him with another wink. "You enjoy yourself, honey. Try not to get into trouble while you're here."

"I make no promises." Although Marshall wasn't one for trouble. At least, he hadn't been until recently. It seemed trouble didn't want to leave him alone anymore. Most of his trouble in life had come from women, the latest of which, in a long line of mistakes, had drawn him into a fistfight in the hall at work that earned him this mental break holiday.

When Marshall turned back to his uncle, the older man stood in the middle of the three little ladies, entertaining them with what was surely one of his usual off-color jokes. They were laughing as Marshall approached and handed off the cup of black coffee.

"Got this for you," he said unnecessarily.

"Well, darlings, I guess that's my cue," Jack told them. He rested his free hand on the back of Birdie's stool and gripped his coffee with the other. "The young-un is anxious to get his ghost on."

"Your uncle told us about your plans for investigating Seafoam House," the middle lady commented. Hattie? Oddly, she was the only one *not* wearing a hat.

Marshall wasn't really in the mood to discuss his plans. Instead, he sent them a smile. "*So* many plans. But we've really got to be going. My mom is expecting us back in time for…" God, what time was it, even? Not even noon yet! "Anyway, it was lovely to meet you. I'm sure I'll be seeing you."

He and Jack made their way toward the door, unaware of the scrutiny their backsides received.

"That poor man needs a taste of love," Trixie said, lowering her reading glasses to watch Marshall walk out the door. "Badly."

Birdie licked her lips. "I wouldn't mind being the one to give it to him."

Hattie replied with a scoff. "Not *him*, you old chucklehead. The nephew."

"Poor boy looks like he never sees the sun. You see how pale he is?" Trixie shook her head and clucked her tongue at the same time. "He didn't even want to try the Café Amour. Although I'm happy to see Eva take the initiative with him. If she hadn't, I would have stepped in. I had my eye on the situation."

"You know, I have the perfect match for him," Hattie said, stroking her chin, deep in thought. "Someone he will *never* expect. Someone who will turn his entire world upside down." She lowered her chin as she stared at her compatriots.

The three women shared another long look. "Are you thinking what I'm thinking?"

"Oh my goodness. Yes. She's perfect!" Birdie clapped her wrinkled palms together. "It's meant to be."

The sun was setting and Marshall knew he wouldn't have much more time to calibrate his instruments before full dark. It would take another day for him to get the generator he needed for lights in the living room, since the power company was unwilling to comply with his request to turn the electricity on because he didn't own the place.

He'd shipped most of his equipment ahead prior to his

arrival, but there were more gadgets in his luggage that he'd brought from home. He'd tried to pack them so that TSA wouldn't take offense, but of course he'd been stuck in line at the airport going over things with the agents for a good hour before his flight. The energy detector now in his hands was something he'd put together himself and could fit in his pocket. Completely portable and able to run on AA batteries. And it worked. It was his proudest geek moment.

He had the key code to the lockbox on his phone, sent ahead by the lady he'd spoken to in the mayor's office. He'd also taken the time before he arrived to contact the proper authorities regarding his research on the place. No one had objected.

Marshall didn't want to break into the house on Seafoam Street like a common vandal. He preferred to go through the proper channels to ensure he was welcome. Now he had access to the key to prove it.

Carefully pressing in the numbers, the bottom of the lockbox popped out and he fished around until he had the key in hand. It fit snugly in the old door lock, but a can of lubricant spray would have done wonders because the lock was rusty, didn't want to budge. Marshall threw his weight into it and bruised his shoulder in the process. Finally, the lock gave way and he shoved against rusted hinges and a warped threshold to get the door open enough to pass through.

Drawing in a breath in the foyer brought with it the scents of dust and mold and neglect. Moisture had snuck in, through the roof more than likely, and taken up residence in the walls. The place must have been nice once upon a time, he thought, turning in a circle. The ceiling was high, a thread-work of cracks showing in the plaster. It was the kind of space that could have comfortably held ornate plush furniture in a bygone era. Now it was empty except for a cluster of dirty rags, a scattering of dried leaves courtesy of a broken window pane or three, and the occasional discarded soda can or snack wrapper, along with the pervasive smell of decay.

As it was, Seafoam House stood out on the street even with the foundation cracking and the roof threatening to cave in. A two-story thing of beauty albeit with peeling paint and rotting wood. Marshall was going to enjoy ferreting out its secrets.

The sensor he gripped gave a single beep. A low but definite reading.

"Whoa, there," he said softly to break the silence. Head angled, he glanced around for anything interesting that could potentially have set off the instrument. Nothing. He held up the energy detector, turning in a slow circle and watching the indicator until he could pinpoint the direction where the signal was strongest.

He stalked toward the kitchen, his footfalls heavy, the instrument in his hand beeping madly the closer he got. Excitement rippled through him and with his free hand he fumbled for the camera he had slung around his neck. This could be it. His big break. Real and tangible evidence that—

He collided with a solid mass. Warm, solid, unexpected. *Breathing.*

Marshall, never one for hysterics, gave in to a stifled yelp.

CHAPTER THREE

"I'm not sure if you heard," Jay Bowen, assistant park manager, began, thumbs hooked through his belt loops. "Someone is here to investigate the old Seafoam House."

Spring's ears perked up immediately. "Ooh, tell me more," she insisted. Her hands folded on the desk as she gave Jay her complete attention. "I didn't realize anyone was interested in it anymore. We haven't had an honest to goodness paranormal team come in to investigate since my first year here."

Jay shrugged. "It doesn't seem this person is part of a team. More of a part-time hobbyist, from what I gather. You know how the Hens can be. Sometimes they mix up their information. Oh, and here's your smoothie."

"Thanks." Spring leaned closer, gripping the tropical smoothie Jay had picked up for her from the coffee shop. "Hobbyist, huh? Well, we get those all the time. Maybe they'll get the thrill they're seeking."

Something she understood all too well. And she did know how Hattie, Trixie, and Birdie could be when it came to information.

Still, she was intrigued. Maybe this time she'd finally have someone to talk to, someone who would appreciate her penchant for the paranormal. Who could give her the stimulating conversation she craved.

Someone who wouldn't run screaming at the tiniest noises in a haunted house in the dead of night. *Thanks, Mecca.*

"Some kind of professor from New York. And related to Jack Beegle," Jay continued.

"The crotchety fisherman who always seems to know where to get the best catch? Yikes." Spring shook her head, taking a sip through her straw. Yeah, she'd heard stories about him too, about how he'd wasted many years searching for mermaids when clearly there were none to be found. "Jack is obsessed with mermaids. I wonder if this guy is the same. But with ghosts, of course."

"I never said it was a guy."

Spring blinked and realized she'd gotten ahead of herself. "You didn't?"

"Nope." Jay laughed, his fingers now tangling in his flamingo-pink belt. Not exactly park uniform regulation, but he liked to push the boundaries of fashion, adorning drab khaki and olive with bright socks and accessories. The park manager had long since given up on admonishing Jay on his choice of apparel. "You've been single for too long. Now you're daydreaming about men," Jay continued.

"I always daydream. About men and otherwise. *Obviously.*"

"Anyway, I know your attachment to the old place, so I wanted to give you a heads-up. Maybe whoever it is will want a volunteer to help them."

"Have they spoken to the town officials?" Spring tucked a lock of dark hair behind her ear, nibbling on the straw stuck in her smoothie. "I wonder if there are permits involved with this kind of thing. Having only gone the B&E route, myself."

"Well, whatever is required, I'm sure he's already taken care of it. Yes, *he.* Why don't you go insert yourself into the situation, be nosy, and find out more? You're so good at that." Jay laughed again when Spring eagerly jumped out of her chair. "Geez, woman, not right this minute! You have a job to do."

He was right, of course. Mecca would *kill* her if she flaked out on her duties again. She'd taken too many personal days lately.

For the last four years since relocating to the area, Spring had worked in the Cinnamon Bay State Park as the assistant camp director for Camp Lionheart But she had *enjoyed* it for the last year, after the newest camp director and her best friend Mecca Raleigh–Lewis moved to town. Working with the camp kids was a challenge, and since Mecca came on board last summer, they had been able to work together— along with Mecca's husband Carter, who managed the park— to get bigger and better grants to extend the camp operations outside the regular summer months.

The local kids loved the added opportunities. Community involvement was up by fifteen percent and they had plans to expand even further the following year. Right now they ran day programs only instead of overnights, which left them more time to plan and write grants. It was much easier with the protocols Mecca had installed since taking over last July. But it left Spring itching for a day off now and again.

She wondered...if she could push her way through a few sheets of paperwork, maybe she could take off early and see what was going on with the Seafoam House investigation.

Talk about letting personal interests impact work!

Spring didn't care. Two hours later, she'd finished most of what she'd intended to do for the day. Jay didn't even look up from his desk when she tried to slip past.

"Leaving for an early dinner?" he asked innocently.

"Oh sure. Sure." She adjusted her bag over her shoulder. "I'll be back..."

"Eventually," he filled in for her. "Right?"

"Just tell them *something* if they ask."

They probably wouldn't. Spring and Mecca had lived together long enough to know each other inside and out, although they were now in separate residences. The rest of the crew would write her off as flighty like they usually did.

Spring couldn't help the swell of anticipation winding up from the pit of her stomach to her throat. This might be the opportunity of a lifetime. Not that she really expected hard evidence of ghosts. It would be insane to think so. But if she could work with a real honest to goodness investigator…it would certainly take her hobby to the next level.

Crazy to think. And exciting.

She let herself into the Seafoam House property the back way, the way she'd been taught by her girl-friends. There was enough space in the fence big enough for a person to slip through, and a window in the basement left unlocked, carefully hidden behind a bush.

She angled her body inside, quietly made her way upstairs. The investigator might not even be there. Still, she had no qualms about trespassing. Yeah, it was technically trespassing, and she knew it was wrong, but excitement spurred her forward and up into the kitchen. Her eyes adjusting to the different light quality, she didn't see the other person in the room.

Didn't hear or smell him, either, until he was on top of her.

Not literally, unfortunately. The moment she understood that she'd come in contact with an actual human and not a supernatural something-or-other, she could see eyes the color of golden-brown honey. And surprise, he was actually quite young, not the gray hair and tweed jacket older college type she'd imagined.

Oooh, hello Professor McSteamy.

His skin exhibited the soft paleness of a man who stayed indoors for most of his life, but it brought out the brightness of his eyes. His nose was straight, his face on the thin side, his hair long-ish and blond-ish and delicious-ish. Perfect for running her fingers through. Not to mention he had killer shoulders.

Meow.

The man clutched his chest. "Holy crap. I thought you were a ghost."

"Nope, just little ol' me," Spring replied with a large grin. Then watched his shoulders relax. "You must be the guy."

"The *guy?*" But his mouth smiled easily enough when he took her in.

It was definitely a good smile, she decided. A little crooked, harmless, and *potent*. He was a nice-looking man, in a bookish and nerdy sort of way. Academicians were not her usual type, but damn, he'd hooked her instantly.

Her brows drew together. "The college professor the town okayed to investigate this old place? Sorry, I guess I'm not making sense." Her own hand rose to rub at her heart when it began to thump erratically. Had she scared herself and not even noticed? "Maybe I had a little fright myself."

The man paused, staring at her. "There are a million questions buzzing around in my brain but only one I can grab hold of. What are you doing here? I mean...how did you get in? All right, two questions. What are you doing here and how did you get in?"

It wasn't the perfect first meeting. Not that Spring had *planned* for a perfect meeting. She didn't even know the guy. But she wouldn't be denied this opportunity.

"How I got in isn't important. Determined people always find a way, don't you agree?"

He only grunted in reply and looked down at some kind of instrument in his hand when it began to beep insistently.

Nosy, she crept closer and peered over his shoulder at the gadget.

"And I'm here because I'm curious," she added.

He shot her a look over his shoulder. "That I can see."

"I've always been intrigued by this place. Plus I love the whole concept."

"Of what?" His tone was dry, his attention focused on whatever gizmo was in his hand. It apparently wasn't working properly, if the look on his face was any indication.

Her brows lifted. "What do you mean, of what? Of this!" Her arms spread wide.

"You must be an old-house buff, then." He walked out of the kitchen and back toward the foyer, leaving her no choice but to follow. In the process, she got a good sense of the breadth of his shoulders. And the shape of his ass. Nice.

Professor McSexy it is.

"Not really, but I can see how you would think that. No, I meant the process of gathering evidence to finally prove, once and for all, that there is life after death. Spring Astin, by the way. It's a pleasure to meet you."

He turned back to her and blinked, then after a moment an abashed look came over his face. "Sorry. I'm in absent-minded mode, I guess. Plus I think I lost a few years off my life running into you. I'm Marshall Rownan. I got into town this morning."

Yes, a definite pleasure, because the man had an excellent butt. It matched the rest of him. She smiled grandly, and it brought out a similar response from him.

"So you have all the proper permits and permissions and all that, which must mean you probably came prepared for a real honest to goodness investigation, which also must mean you brought lots of scientific equipment to document your findings. How about you let me help you carry in some of your equipment?" she offered. "I'm sure you have a lot more that just that gadget in your hand."

He glanced down at the energy meter and decided to switch it off for the time being. No sense in wasting the batteries. "I do, but it's in my luggage on the front porch. Luggage which has wheels. Your help isn't needed."

Was that a dismissal? Well, she wasn't giving up yet. "I offered, so I want to. Besides, isn't your equipment expensive? Why risk having it stolen? Better bring it inside."

He lifted a brow. "Thieves on Seafoam Street?"

"Well, trespassers anyway." She winked at him. "So how long are you going to be in town, Professor Rownan?" she practically purred.

She couldn't help herself. The man drew her like a giant pizza in front of a person on a diet. She wanted to take a bite right out of him. And lucky for her, she'd been in the middle of a dry spell when it came to acceptable, dateable men.

Spring never liked to deprive herself of male company if she could help it. Lately, with seasonal tourism winding down, pickings had been slim and she'd been left with locals she either discounted or thought of more as brothers.

None of them were good prospects for romance.

But this one...

"Just for a couple of weeks," Marshall answered absent-mindedly. "It's a forced vacation."

"You mean your wife or girlfriend kicked you out of the house and you needed to get away?"

She hadn't intended to be so forward about it. Still, his very near flush brought heat to her chest. It had been an innocent question. Kind of.

Marshall angled his head as he stared at her. "No girl-friend or wife. *Work.* Apparently, I've been having some issues and they thought a change of scenery would do me good." He glanced away without saying more, although there was clearly more to be said.

She'd pry later.

Spring stepped to the side when he brought several of his

bags through the front door. Like he was moving into the place, she thought. She grabbed the last two satchels and followed him inside.

She jerked her thumb over her shoulder. "This is all you brought?"

"There's more at my house that I haven't dragged over. I wasn't planning on doing a full-scale investigation, at least not initially. It's just...something to keep me busy. Otherwise, it will be me, my mother, and my uncle. I'm not big on family time."

"Who is your uncle?" she asked, despite knowing the answer. It didn't pay to play her hand too soon.

"Jack Beegle. Down at the docks? From what he tells me, he single-handedly provides seafood for the entire town."

She affected a picture of wide-eyed guilelessness. "Oh, man. Yeah, I've had a few run-ins with him. He's either trying too hard to be sweet or he's about as sour as a lemon soaked in vinegar. It could go either way with that guy," she confided. "Depending on his mood."

"You pegged him right." Finally, Marshall straightened and turned his full attention on Spring. The weight of his eyes brought the heat in her chest to the next level and she felt color flush her cheeks.

"What's the matter?" she couldn't help but ask. Hoping she didn't sound choked.

"How did you get in here? And what exactly are you doing here? You never told me."

She debated telling him the truth and then shrugged. "I've been coming in here for years, really. There's a side window that stays unlocked, behind the lilac bush in the back. Pretty well hidden."

"Are you responsible for the..." He gestured to the walls and the crude sayings spray-painted across the peeling wallpaper.

Her eyes widened then narrowed. "Absolutely not. I'm an

investigator like you are. Or maybe I should say a hobbyist. Okay, less than that. I just…I really like the paranormal, okay? Halloween is my favorite time of year." Was she babbling? Hopefully not. "I've been coming here for years because I'm intrigued with anything to do with hauntings. Plus I love the old place. It gives me a good feeling, being here."

It had until her last trip, at least. But things were looking up!

Marshall nodded as if he understood, retrieved the gadget from earlier and turned it on, then lifted the beeping machine toward the staircase. "There are reported to be strange things that happen on Halloween night. Are you familiar with the concept of the Sabbat of Samhain?"

She wanted to be. And might have been on a normal day. Really, she did know, but she couldn't stop staring at his smile, feeling a little goofy and light-headed and a lot more tongue-tied than usual.

"You can tell me about it," she said at last, still staring at him. "I'd love to learn more. Finding a real ghost is on my bucket list."

His expression shifted. Lips pursed, eyes narrowed, and his brows burrowed down toward his nose. "It's getting late. I think I'd better call it a night. I'm going to stow my gear and then lock up behind me."

"Are you sure you don't want me to help?"

"*No*. Thank you."

His answer left very little room to maneuver. Spring knew when she'd been beaten, and if his expression hadn't given her any indication, the dry tone would have. She pasted a smile on her face instead, playing it light. "All right, then. It was really nice to meet you, Marshall. And my offer of help still stands, anytime, so I'm going to give you my phone number."

She scrambled in her pockets for anything she could use to write. And only then realized she was still wearing her work uniform. Yikes. Olive-drab t-shirts and bland khaki shorts did nothing for her complexion. Maybe he liked a woman in uniform? A girl could hope.

"I'm not going to need any help," he asserted, adjusting the camera around his neck. "I'm only here for two weeks."

"Even so. Just in case." When he was not forthcoming with pen or paper, and when she couldn't find anything on her end, Spring went down on her knees and wrote her number in the dust on the floor. Knowing that unless Marshall got the windows open, which wasn't likely tonight, there would be no stiff breeze to blow it away. "Give me a call," she continued. "For work, for pleasure. Maybe even dinner. To show you that not all inhabitants of Cinnamon Bay are kooks, although we might seem that way at first. It was nice to meet you."

He spared her a look and hooked his thumbs around the handles of his bag. "It was nice to meet you as well, Spring. Goodbye."

It was time to take her leave, that was obvious. With nothing more to say, she strolled out the front door, hands in her pockets, like she owned the place.

She ended up not going back to work but spending the rest of the evening at home dreaming about *him*. Fantasizing, more like, because the man checked several boxes in the chemistry area. She was intrigued by his mind, captivated by his face, and wanted to know more about his work besides the few little tidbits he'd given her.

After a fitful night of little sleep, she sauntered out onto the beach early the next morning for a walk and ended up halfway to town before she realized where her legs had taken her. Better to drive, she thought, and turned around to head for the car.

She pulled up in front of the Seafoam Street house and put her car in park. The place was calm, still, and those dirty windows looked out on the street with a blankness befitting abandoned homes.

Spring pushed through the chain-link fence and gate, as

usual, and sauntered up to the front door. The lockbox was back in place. Which meant he wasn't here at the moment.

"Marshall?" she called out anyway.

No answer even when she pounded on the door, nor when she called his name several more times. Spring made her way around the back to her hidden entrance.

Bending down in the dirt, she maneuvered around the lilac bush and pushed against the window.

Locked.

CHAPTER FOUR

His first thought was that Spring would be mad at him for locking the window. Then Marshall ejected that thought from his mind.

What did he care what some nutjob thought of him? She was a stranger, number one. And number two, she was obviously not the sort of woman he needed to get involved with, since her idea of fun involved trespassing, breaking and entering, and thrill-seeking by way of the paranormal. All of which was shared by his crazed ex and none of which he wanted to involve himself with ever again.

They were on his list of no-nos.

Too bad, though, the wishful part of his brain responded. She was a beautiful woman, Spring Astin. The type that made men stop and look twice.

He didn't have time *or* inclination to look twice, no matter what he thought. And no matter that when he closed his eyes that night, he could still see her smile in his memory.

Marshall had spent the last two uncomfortable evenings on his mother's futon in the spare room that doubled for a sewing nook. The little house inland from the boardwalk that she and her brother rented together was small but tidy. A place for everything and everything in its place. There were three bedrooms, two bathrooms, and a common area with a kitchen attached. They weren't the closest to the beach, but it was a nice walk on a cool evening, and his mom took great pleasure in telling him how she'd lost twenty pounds by jogging to the ocean and back every morning, even with the oppressive summer heat.

She didn't need to lose any weight, still maintaining the same figure she'd had in her younger years, but good for her. He'd never jogged anywhere in his life and he didn't plan on starting now.

Staring at the ceiling in the guest room, scratchy cotton sheets at his back, he wondered how he should spend his day. If he were at home then it wouldn't be a question at all. He would get up and make himself a pot of coffee. Brush his teeth, shower, and dart out the door with the entire pot in a container, ready to sustain him through the day.

His morning classes started at nine and lasted until noon, when he allowed himself fifteen minutes to eat lunch before working on his side projects until his next round of classes began at two. At the moment, those projects included a manuscript about haunted houses and how they've shaped communities in a positive way rather than a negative.

Marshall had a sneaking suspicion it would never get read, let alone published.

He glanced over at the clock and noted the time. It was only eight, yet Jack and Emmie were both already out of the house. That left Marshall alone with his thoughts.

He hated what popped up in them.

Killer legs and a smile to match, topped off by lush hair and bedroom eyes.

Uh-oh. He needed to get away. *Fast*.

From experience, Marshall knew that most of the activity at the Seafoam Street house—if there was any—would happen after nightfall, which meant he should use his day to catch up on rest and notes. Especially if he wanted to pull an all-nighter, which seemed inevitable at the moment.

He knew what his colleagues would say if they knew he had undertaken yet another project. They'd tell him to slow down. To stop running away from the demons in his mind and focus on taming them rather than becoming buried in another new project.

But the haunting on Seafoam Street called out to him and he pushed those other voices aside until he could mute them entirely.

He remembered their faces two weeks ago when he'd been particularly upset about Hannah, his ex-girlfriend, and had channeled his aggravation and frustration toward an unsuspecting freshman. The same incident that had landed him in hot water with the dean. The looks they had given him. Like he was a ticking time bomb about to blow at any moment.

Did none of them *know* him, or recognize that his usual self-control had been utterly tested to the limit? He wasn't the type of person to react in such a way without cause. Without *good* cause.

It seemed they didn't care.

Instead of dwelling on that, he got in the car his mother was letting him borrow and headed to the boardwalk. He'd indulge in a cup or two of coffee, take in some of the local sights including the bookstore, and then go home and do a little writing before he took a nap.

This vacation stuff is a bitch, he thought with a rogue smile.

Marshall found a place to park near a bar with neon lights flashing even in the daytime. Never one for drinking, he kept the possibility in his back pocket should the need arise for a little numbness—if family time became too much for him to bear. Then he slathered on some sunscreen before exiting the car. If he wanted to keep his Casper-level pale skin then he needed to take the necessary precautions. Skin cancer was no joke.

The heat hit him first, landing squarely on his head and shoulders and feeling like it pushed him down several inches into the pavement. If it was this hot in October, how might the weather be during June and July? He didn't really want to find out.

With the transitional lenses in his eyeglasses finally adjusting to the brightness, Marshall stepped onto the boardwalk and turned toward the ocean. Okay, a guy could get used to a view like this, he conceded. The enormous expanse of water loomed ahead, with blue-and-green waves crashing on a sandy shore. Scrubby green grass and shrubs covered the dunes and danced in the wind. The weather-beaten boardwalk led from shops to sea.

"Oh, you there! Jack's nephew! God, Trixie, what was his name again? Mitchell!"

Taking a deep breath did nothing to prepare him for the one meeting he hadn't wanted to repeat. "Marshall," he corrected the trio of older ladies as he walked forward.

"Yes, Marshall. Isn't that what I said?" The one with the tan beret—otherwise known as the withered apple of his uncle's eye—gestured toward the others. "I'm pretty sure I said Marshall. But I didn't see your uncle this morning. He usually likes to stop in for a cup and conversation. Is something the matter?"

The three of them had gathered on a park bench outside of the coffee shop, looking exactly like the quirky and eccentric senior citizens they were. Each was made up with an assortment of makeup, rouge, hats, and skirts that belonged to years gone by. And they stared at him like hungry wolves rather than humans.

"I can't speak for where Jack goes," Marshall answered kindly. "I can only tell you he was up with the sun and out the door quickly."

"Ah, he's a sly one, that Jackie boy." The woman who'd spoken earlier wiggled her finger.

The one without a hat eyed Marshall up and down. Hattie? "And where are you off to this morning, young man? Out to catch the eye of a pretty girl, surely."

He'd never had grandparents around to smother him with advice. Which meant he was at a unique disadvantage on how to handle the situation.

Keep calm, they can smell fear, he told himself.

Marshall shook his head. "No pretty girls for me. I'm just taking in the sights and seeing what else the Cinnamon Bay boardwalk has to offer besides great coffee."

This had the intended effect and they all glowed under the compliment. "Well, if you like ice cream, Bay Freeze has the best cones in the county. You should head over that way and grab a bite for yourself," Hattie stated proudly.

With the sun beating down on him, he had to admit it wasn't the worst idea he'd heard. His stomach growled in evidence that he'd skipped breakfast. "I might head down that way. Thanks for the advice."

"Not so fast there, sweetheart." Swifter than lightning, the sweet grandmotherly middle woman with curling white hair was off the bench with her claws fastened around his wrist. Holding Marshall in place better than iron shackles.

"Um—"

"Jack hasn't told us that much about you," she said, cutting him off. Then dropped her gaze coyly to his feet and slowly raised her head, her eyes raking him from toes to top. "You're a professor, eh?"

Marshall bristled under the physical contact and the blatant examination but knew it wouldn't bode well for him— or his uncle—if he rudely broke away. So he endured it. "Yes, I teach engineering at NYU."

"Ooh, prestigious! You're going to be the catch of the town if you stay here much longer."

His expression soured despite his intention to be polite. "I'm no one's *catch* and I'm really not interested in what people have to say about me." Then his eyes went wide when she linked her arm through his and led him down the boardwalk, with the other two moving in on his other side.

Trapped!

"A professor *and* an amateur ghost hunter." The one who had a decided crush on his uncle—Birdie?—toddled next to him with sure feet. "We don't get many people with your varied interests around here."

"I can only think of one other person who shares your passion," hatless Hattie added. "But like you said, you're not interested in romance. It would be a waste of an introduction despite your spooky shared interest."

The third one chimed in. "Halloween is just around the corner. It's a *time* for spooks and thrills."

Marshall wasn't sure where they were going with this conversation. Even in his wildest imaginings, he couldn't guess how they would link it all together. "Yes, Halloween is always exciting," he managed to say, nearly losing his balance when the trio veered him out of the way of an oncoming mom with a stroller.

"It's a big to-do around here," Hattie said with a decisive dip of her chin. "Many people get into it wholeheartedly. Decorating, trick-or-treating, dressing up in costume. In fact, the boardwalk does a spectacular job, with each business decorating their storefront and giving out candy to children. We used to have a haunted house, too, to raise money for local charities. A *real* haunted house. Much like the one you're investigating. Isn't that right, dear?"

He let them steer him down the boardwalk, the Hens flanking him like three indomitable escapees from a retirement home. "I—"

"Think you'll have a costume picked out by then?"

He chuckled. "I'm not sure I'm the right age for a costume," he answered, his head reeling.

"Oh, there's no age requirement for costumes, you know. Well, that's all right. There's still time. Might I suggest you go as yourself? The *academic* look is always a draw for young ladies. Until next time, Professor Rownan." Hattie sent him on his way with a pat on the shoulder.

"And say hello to that devil of an uncle of yours, the next time you cross his path," Birdie called out.

Marshall waved goodbye until his wrist ached and glanced up to find himself in front of the ice cream shop. Bay Freeze. The three little women disappeared back in the direction they'd come, probably bursting through the front door of the coffee shop like a tornado to return to their roosts near the front counter.

He shook his head, meaning to turn around and walk in the opposite direction toward the bookstore, his stomach filled with the half a pot of coffee he'd ingested before leaving the house. The ice cream could wait until he'd explored the bookshelves and purchased some reading material.

Then Marshall stopped cold.

He stared at the tall, attractive brunette with legs long enough to take her to any runway in the world and make a splash. She leaned over the boardwalk railing to chat with a young couple passing by on the sand below.

Spring.

His insides gave a lurch, as if his solar plexus were being magnetically drawn to her, and he nearly followed through on the inclination. Then he remembered locking the window...

Well, shit. She wasn't going to be happy with him if they came face to face. Perhaps he could slip away unnoticed before she turned and—

No such luck. Spring's gaze fell in his direction and her casual smile dropped into an even, thin line. Oh, she wasn't happy to see him. Not even a little bit.

Marshall contemplated turning and running as fast as he could in the opposite direction, but he figured she would catch him easily enough. With those legs, she'd be on him in no time.

So he stood and locked his knees in preparation for whatever she would have to say to him. None of it good. Because he knew from the angle of her spine and the set of her shoulders, there was going to be something. And he was man enough to take it.

He hoped.

Spring said a breezy goodbye to the couple, then approached him with long, easy strides. He couldn't help but admire how gracefully she moved, almost feline. And was that a smile on her face? Or a feral, predatory grin? He felt himself heat up despite the icy displeasure in her eyes.

She stopped two feet from him, crossed her arms over her chest. *Not* where his attention wanted to be drawn at the moment. "Professor Rownan."

He swallowed. "Ms. Astin."

"What are you doing here?"

A simple question, so why couldn't he answer it? "I—I… Ice cream," he managed. And glanced up at the Bay Freeze sign, hoping she'd believe this was his destination all along.

Apparently not. "You locked me out of the house," Spring accused.

Marshall shoved his hands in his pockets and began walking down the boardwalk, aiming for the short steps leading down to the beach. Unfazed, Spring turned and kept pace with him. He watched her from the corner of his eye, alert to her mood but also because he couldn't keep his eyes off her. Ogling wasn't polite, especially since he had no interest in her whatsoever. But he was only human. And she had an amazingly beautiful body.

Too bad her attitude couldn't match. Not at the moment, anyway.

She slanted him a look. "You aren't even going to answer me?"

"I'm not sure what you want me to say," Marshall responded easily. "Was that even a question? Because you obviously know the answer to it. Yes, I locked you out of the house. You and anyone else who might be using that window."

Her laughter was about as dry as her mood. "You have quite a lot of nerve, Professor Rownan," she said through gritted teeth.

"Look, I understand your fascination with tales of haunted houses. I even understand your wanting to talk to me about paranormal events," he said, hoping he had enough supplication in his tone to appease her while still stating the truth. "But I don't think it's safe for you or anyone else to be in that house. Not anymore. Not only is the foundation crumbling in places, but there's also black mold coming from a leak in the roof, which also means rotten wood that can look deceptively solid until you put weight on it and fall through. Not to mention unfounded gossip about paranormal events can sometimes grab hold of the unwary or weak-minded and mark them with a terrifying psychological experience."

"Wait, what? Now you sound like a professor, Professor. Don't take it upon yourself to determine what is best for *me*. Do you think I'm scared of ghosts or mold? *Neither* scares me, Marshall, and neither does your tone."

She'd seen right through him. "Well, I'm glad to hear it. But I'd rather you stay out of the house. At least while I'm there." Voice cheerful, face open if somewhat sheepish, he shrugged. "Do it as a personal favor to me."

He'd been thinking of her safety, of course. Thinking of the way she must have to angle her slender body through the fence and avoid the sharp metal points where the chain-link had been cut. He thought of the way the steps creaked and groaned on the porch and how, at any minute, the wood might give way.

Then he thought of the problems she'd bring on his head if she were to get hurt.

"Why should I? After the way you pushed me out the other night, and finding the house locked tight the next morning..." She trailed off, her head shaking and her long dark hair flowing out behind her in the warm ocean breeze.

"What?"

Wisps of hair flew across her heart-shaped face, hiding her expression from him. "Nothing. There's nothing more to say to you, I guess. You seem like the type to make up his mind and stick to it. Which I normally find appealing in men but somehow on you it rubs me the wrong way."

Marshall sucked in a breath. She wanted to smack him upside the head, and probably would if he gave her a chance. Despite that, he smiled. Spring was definitely full of sass. He found he liked her go-get-'em attitude after all.

It really was a shame he wasn't interested in her. A damn shame. She was the best-looking woman he'd come across in months, if not longer. Possibly years. And she didn't seem like she was willing to take any of his shit. If he wasn't such an irritating asshole, then they might have been able to enjoy an entirely different set of extracurricular activities during his short stay in Cinnamon Bay.

Instead, he was going to have to keep his attention on work and focus on his project. It wouldn't be easy, but it was the whole point of him coming here. Right?

"I can be swayed occasionally," he countered, stopping to lean on the railing and stare at the ocean. "In fact, if we were back in New York right now and you were taking classes, I'd be so impressed with your tenacity I'd ask you to be one of my assistants."

Tenacity? That made her sound like a pit bull. He kept his

gaze on the ocean waves rhythmically breaking on the sand to avoid the reproach surely written on her face.

Spring laughed, and when he whirled to face her, a perfectly gorgeous flush rose to her cheeks. "What you're saying is that you like the way I operate and you want me for your assistant."

"Well, sure, I'd hire you," he hurried to say to smooth things over.

She turned, stunning him by wrapping her arms around his shoulders. "Great! What time should I meet you at Seafoam House tonight?"

Marshall blinked. Blinked again. Knew he'd been caught in a trap of his own making. "Come again?"

"I know you're going back there tonight. When? I'll come with you and be your assistant. You just said you'd hire me." She broke contact and waved when he opened his mouth to protest. "Don't worry, you don't have to actually pay me. I'll do this for free. As my way of saying welcome to town. Plus I'm familiar. The house knows me. And this is kind of my thing."

"You're not coming with me," he said firmly before she could clamp down on the idea like a dog with a meaty bone. Pit bull, indeed. "Didn't we just talk about this?"

"You did, but I never agreed to stay away."

He started to brush her off. He *wanted* to brush her off and would have on any other day. He didn't work well with others. Still...

"One night," he warned. Unable to stop himself.

Her smile was dazzling. "One night? Deal."

Why did he get the feeling she was only telling him what he wanted to hear? "Let's just see how it goes. We might not even work well together. But I'm going to run some tests tonight and I could use the help." He shoved his hair back away from his face, suddenly feeling too hot. "It always goes better when there are two—"

Spring let out a whoop and launched herself at him. "Thank you, Marshall!"

Before he knew what was happening, the entire length of her body was pressing along the front of his body. And suddenly her lips fell on his.

Damn. He hadn't expected a hand grenade to go off in his chest.

The instant she'd pressed her mouth to his for a brief kiss, the rest of the world turned off and his insides detonated. In the best possible way, of course. His heart gave an almost painful thud against his ribs when she nibbled his lips, teasing them.

"What do you think you're doing?" he asked, dumbfounded, when she leaned back. His voice came out strangled. Husky. He couldn't take his eyes off of her no matter how loudly his mind screamed at him to do so.

"I'm giving in," she replied, her body moving closer, and closer still, until she was practically imprinted against him.

Spring was everywhere. Surrounding him. Taking him under and enveloping him in her scent, her softness. Her arms were around his neck. His automatically closed around her, his heart turning over even when he knew he should move away. Do something, anything, to break the spell she was weaving around him.

Her touch was compelling and the world around them went suddenly hazy. Her mouth feathered across his cheek to his temple, down to the corner of his lips. Marshall groaned and deepened the kiss despite his better judgment. He was torn in two, knowing he should run far and fast from this woman, yet also knowing this was so *perfect*.

His tongue slipped in through her open lips, stroking across the roof of her mouth in a rasping caress. Spring groaned in response, which sent heat spiraling down to his nether regions. He didn't even care that they were in public. His fingers curled into her shirt to keep her close to him.

"I want to say thank you," Spring murmured when they broke apart a second time. Her lips lightly bruised and pink. Luscious.

"Hmm?"

"For letting me help you." She spoke quietly. Almost soberly.

He blinked and watched her eyelashes sweep down and those damn pink lips curve in a grin. Tapping him on the shoulder, Spring used his confusion to step away from him, adjusting her disheveled blouse.

"I..." His brain refused to engage.

"I'll meet you at the house at nine. Don't be late." She pecked a kiss against his cheek before turning and walking in the opposite direction, her backside swaying enticingly.

His vision blurred and the rest of him felt like a blank canvas. Waiting for her to come back to splash color on his otherwise empty world.

Had he thought her harmless earlier? It seemed a strange thing to call her now. Marshall managed to stagger a few steps toward his parked car, then had to lower himself onto an empty bench, drawing in a deep breath.

A few minutes, he figured. A few minutes to get his legs under him and then he'd go home. And prepare to see her again. He didn't expect to get his rational mind back until he did.

CHAPTER FIVE

*S*pring made it a point to not only arrive early at Seafoam House but to have a freshly made batch of sugar cookies with her. Not for any other reason than she'd had the itch to bake them and made too many.

Or so she told herself.

There was still thirty minutes before she'd told Marshall they'd meet. She believed in being prompt. She also believed in creating a path to a man's heart through his stomach. Thus the cookies, if she were to be completely honest. Besides, it was always better to face a long night with a little food as a pick-me-up.

And yes, she had backup excuses for everything.

Luckily, it was Saturday and Mecca gave her the weekend off, after much pleading and cajoling. It was just as well. Spring was getting to the point in her life where it was difficult to stay out all night and make it in to work the next day without feeling eighty years old.

She leaned against the porch railing until she felt it shift in the wrong direction, then hurried to right herself. Adjusting the set of her loose—but not *too* loose—green shirt, Spring set the cookies down and tightened her ponytail.

Nothing to do now except wait. Wait as she'd done this morning when Hattie, Trixie, and Birdie had caught her and told her to stand by the ice cream shop while they went off to grab the book they'd promised to bring her, the one from their last book club meeting.

They never had brought it, obviously forgetting about her, but she'd run into Marshall, so it wasn't all bad. Not bad at all, in fact, because...

It had ended with a kiss.

She'd been the one to initiate it, of course. Spring had learned long ago to never say no when an opportunity arose. The opportunity had certainly presented itself then. Wow, the man knew what he was doing, once he got warmed up. And the way he'd grabbed her...it made her knees weak, and if he hadn't kept hold of her during the kiss, she might have floated away.

She still felt a little weak-kneed, just reliving the moment.

A few minutes later, Marshall pulled up to the curb and parked his borrowed Ford beside the rotting white fence. He rounded the hood bleary-eyed and wearing a comfortable pair of sweatpants along with a t-shirt from the college where he worked. Spring felt her heart flip over at the sight of him tousled. As if he'd just risen from bed. She could get used to that view.

This was a new side of *Professor McSexy*, she decided. A side that put her in mind of cool winter days when the wind blew in from the ocean bringing flakes of snow and it was better to curl up on the couch with something hot. Preferably the teacher in question.

She could picture it now and struggled to keep her mind from delving down, down into the gutter where she desperately wanted to go. With him specifically. But Lord knew he was far from willing.

Although the kiss *had* given her a slender thread of hope.

"Hey there, you," she called out when he got a little closer, her lips lifted in an easy grin. "You ready to do some investigating tonight? I made cookies."

Marshall grunted, as close to a greeting or a thank-you as she would get, and swung past her with the keys in his hand.

She kept the container pressed against her hip and followed him to the door. Waited patiently while he found the right key and opened the rusted lock. He wasn't keen on making conversation, either, if his lack of eye contact told her anything. "O-o-o-kay. I guess you aren't in the mood for cookies."

"I'm in the mood to get this started. I'm anxious to see what I come up with." He pushed his shoulder against the door when it jammed, using his body weight to get it open. The hinges squealed and the warped door grated against the wooden floor. At once the scents of age, mold, and dust assaulted her nostrils.

"I think you mean what *we* come up with," Spring corrected.

Crossing the room, Marshall stopped in front of a card table he'd erected earlier, the top already laden with an assortment of electronic equipment and a slim laptop. He had balls leaving his equipment here, Spring gave him that, although now that he'd fortified the entrances, there was less of a chance of trespassers bothering his stuff.

"I should warn you before we get started," he stated, his back turned to her, "I have a reputation for not working well with others. It's nothing personal."

He wasn't facing her so she didn't have a chance to see his facial expression when he growled out the sentiment. But she refused to be deterred.

"Are you trying to scare me off? Because I'll tell you, I don't scare easily. I'm one of the few people who have actually spent the entire night here in the house." She lifted her chin to stare at the ceiling, cracks in the plaster evidence of age and water damage. "In fact I may be the only person.

Everyone else has either chickened out or refused. Or lied about it."

"I'm not trying to scare you. I just want you to know that if I'm short with you, it's nothing personal," he repeated.

"Ah. I get it. You're trying to excuse your bad behavior right off the bat," Spring replied. Then, needing something to do besides stand there feeling foolish, she set the container of cookies down on the last free space on the table, staring at him.

Marshall glanced over once, met her eyes, then focused on booting up the laptop. "No, I'm not. I know how women can be. You take *every* little thing personally."

"Well, *I* usually don't, but if you keep saying shit like that I might." This time her tone did not come out as breezy. "I don't like the way you're talking to me, Professor Rownan."

Especially not after the shared lip-lock hours earlier. She'd heard of men blowing hot and cold, but damn, this took things to a whole new level.

He ran his hands through his hair and scratched slightly. Not bothered by her statement in the least. "Can you unpack the bag to your left? I want to get the machines hooked up. Have you ever worked an EMF meter before?"

Spring gritted her teeth and did as he asked. "Just because I'm not a professional at this doesn't mean I can't figure it out. I'm a camp counselor. I work with children. I can handle pretty much anything."

"You work with children?" Marshall asked, turning to her. "So do I. Ages eighteen and older."

"Ha! Got you beat. Twelve and younger. They are the devil's spawn. All of them."

It helped smooth her ruffled feathers when his lips raised in a tiny smile. "I can only imagine how horrifying that is. Now tell me, since you're so familiar with the landmark, I want to know the history of the house and the area. Something I haven't read already before I got here, and trust me, I've read a lot of material on the old place."

"How am I supposed to know what you've read and what you haven't?" Spring followed him through the living room where he grabbed a box of some unidentifiable small equipment and plopped it into her hands, then motioned for her to follow him toward the staircase.

"Then just assume I know nothing and go from there."

"Not so hard," she muttered under her breath. Then straightened with a grin when his shoulders snapped tight. He'd heard her. "Okay, well, Seafoam House was apparently built with timbers from a shipwreck salvaged off the beach. Some people even say that the timbers belong to the lost ship of the pirate Leo "Lionheart" DeVane."

"Go on," Marshall directed as he began to remove a few of those gadgets from her box and position them at strategic points on the staircase.

"Built in 1850, the place has had multiple owners but none who stayed more than a few years until finally the town bought it for historical purposes."

"Why wouldn't anyone stay more than a few years?"

Was he just keeping her occupied? Surely he'd already done the research on the history of the house. If she didn't know better, she'd think he was getting a kick out of listening to her tell the story. Spring decided it didn't hurt to indulge him. She knew how to weave a tale. She considered herself a regular bard. If only her experience with scary stories told around a campfire could go on her resume...

"Because no owners were brave enough to live in it. Unexplained noises, disembodied voices, flashes of light, moving shadows. Some say they felt distinct presences on the second floor and there are reports of seeing the figures of a young girl and an older gentleman. None of these have been thoroughly documented, however."

"Until now." Marshall held his sensor aloft and searched

for changes in the signal. "None of them have been thoroughly documented *until now*."

Was it wrong that it gave her a little thrill to repeat "Until now"? She hid her smile. "But of course you would already know this," Spring stated, propping the box on her hip. "You would have learned as much about the location site as you could before even coming here, which means you've already researched the history and know all about the legends and myths. You've probably interviewed everyone involved with the house—everyone still alive, at least—including residents on the street. Plus—"

He was close enough that he could place a hand over her mouth to shush her. "You're only half right."

"About which part?" she asked, voice muffled from the contact.

"I haven't interviewed the neighbors yet." Marshall winked before turning around and breaking contact. He checked his gadget again, moving slowly up the staircase, and every time it emitted a high-pierced signal he'd stop and attach some kind of sensor to the wall.

Curious, Spring trailed him, wondering what to do with herself besides box-bearer. It looked to her like he was setting up some kind of alarms that might alert them to the presence of anything coming down the stairs. But he didn't ask for her help. Hadn't he said he needed an assistant? Did holding a box qualify? At this rate, she'd simply be there to look pretty. Which was flattering, but a little unsatisfying.

"Why don't you tell me a little about yourself, Professor —" *McSexy*. She cut herself off to keep from saying her private nickname for him. No need to air that yet.

Marshall threw a sharp glance in her direction. "What do you want to know?"

"Oh, you know. The basics. Where you're from, what you do for fun. Any hobbies besides ghost hunting?" *And do you believe in love at first sight?*

Because by God, she'd never been a believer before, but the burning in her chest when she looked at him was enough to convince her otherwise. Too powerful to be heartburn, too consistent to be indigestion, and growing in strength the longer she was around Marshall.

It was a *feeling*, and Spring had long ago learned to trust her feelings. Feelings were like little nudges in a certain direction. Not to be ignored.

Heeding her feelings had kept her from making a few too many mistakes in her past. If something felt wrong, then it probably was.

Alternatively, if something felt *right*...

"I'm from New York, born and raised. Happily employed by NYU in the engineering department for the last five years."

Something about the way he said it led her to believe it wasn't really happy employment. "And they let you take time off in the middle of the semester? That's great!"

His response was slow in coming. "Actually, it was more like forced leave. Like I told you before. A vacation sanctioned by the dean."

"Forced vacation? Ah, are you a workaholic, then? Burning yourself out by working the candle from both ends? Think that's the expression."

"I can be a workaholic, yes, but that's not the problem. My coworkers were starting to get worried about my mental health."

Spring scrunched her forehead in thought. "Mental health like you're going to go psycho on me?" She took a step back down the staircase. "Or like you are burned out and need a break?"

"They'd tell you the former. I'll admit to the latter. The story is a bit more complicated than I'd like to get into, seeing as we don't know each other that well." He paused again, lips pursed in anticipation of saying more, then he shook his head.

"And here you are *working* on your break," she commented.

"This time it's something I really enjoy doing, for an actual hobby I mean."

"You don't like your work? I thought you said you were happily employed."

His eyes narrowed when he turned to face her. "I don't like where this conversation is going. It feels incredibly one-sided."

"Ah, well, let me fix that for you." Spring set the box down on the stairs and removed the last two sensors from it. She held them up, ready for whenever Marshall wanted another one. "I love my job. I'm an associate director for Camp Lionheart located in the Cinnamon Bay State Park."

"So how did a nice camp director like you get involved in breaking into haunted houses?"

She chuckled and swung her hands for emphasis. "I'd *like* to tell you I love Halloween for the candy, but..."

Marshall grunted. "I know. And can you be careful with those, please? They're rather delicate. And expensive."

Spring clutched the gadgets to her chest protectively. "I just naturally gravitate toward spooky things. I love the decorations, watching scary movies, haunted houses. The fun fake ones *and* the ones that are actually haunted. It started when I was young and I watched an old movie called *The Haunting*. Then my mom bought me the book to read—you know, *The Haunting of Hill House* by Shirley Jackson—and I was hooked."

He gave her such a warm look of surprise and appreciation that it had her blushing. "Classic. I knew I had the right person for the job here, even though it's only for one night. Then we'll— Whoa!" Marshall paused when the electronic thingamajig in his hand began to beep erratically.

"What does that mean?" Spring asked eagerly, leaning closer.

"It means there's been a significant change in ambient temperature. Spring!" The sensors along the staircase began to flash and beep, including the ones she held.

He hurried up to the landing. "Cold spots everywhere. I'll bet EMF is off the charts We need the EMF meter. And the EVP recorder. Go, grab them! Hurry!"

Spring's heart jumped into her throat and stayed there for the next ten minutes while she scrambled to fetch the electronic gadgets he wanted and Marshall scrambled to record data as events occurred. Blood pounded through her veins and her pulse echoed in her ears, not to mention that every fine hair on her body stood on end.

"Have you ever experienced anything like this?" Spring asked him breathlessly.

He shook his head, eyes glittering in the hazy light. "Nothing this substantial. At this rate, we'll have enough data to support a full investigation—which means grant money— and with any luck, validation for publication."

She wasn't entirely sure exactly what he meant, but his excitement was palpable. Contagious. She clapped her hands together. Then froze in shock when Marshall grabbed her around the midsection. He spun her around in a circle until the heels of her shoes nearly knocked into the crumbling wallpaper.

"We did it!"

She couldn't help but laugh when he set her down on her feet. Pride swelled in her chest and she stared up into Marshall's face, her eyes tracing a path down from his eyes to his lips. She felt herself leaning in when he took a step back to break their connection.

"We did it," he repeated, tugging at his shirt. "But this is just the first tiny step on the path. We need to do a lot more testing before we come to any verifiable conclusions."

Spring forced herself to nod instead of giving in to the kernel of disappointment she felt. Disappointment that he hadn't kissed her again.

Refusing to dwell on that, she cast him a sultry but happy smile and jerked her chin toward the stairs. "Well then, let's get to work, Professor."

CHAPTER SIX

They stayed in the house longer than he'd projected, working in tandem until nearly three in the morning. He'd eaten half the cookies and filled up most of the brand-new notebook he'd bought for this purpose before the grit in his eyes turned to sandpaper and he walked Spring out the front door, locking it behind them.

Marshall forced one foot in front of the other as he bundled Spring into her car, then watched until her rear lights faded.

They'd come far tonight.

Not only had the results from their testing gone way better than expected, but they worked well together. *Too well*, the snarky part of his subconscious goaded. And when things went this well, it usually signaled a fluke.

He didn't trust anything that was too easy.

Plus he definitely had his hands full with her, that was for sure. He'd barely been able to keep up with their conversation and her uncanny knack for verbal sparring. Now if he could just figure out what to do with her...

Marshall knew what Spring wanted *him* to do, he thought tiredly, dragging himself to the spare room in his mother's house and trying not to wake anyone in the process. Spring wanted him to ask her out on a date. She'd made her intentions—and her interest—clear enough.

Which would be a whirlwind adventure. He knew it, could sense it. They'd have fun together, but he wasn't interested in two weeks of fun before he went back to New York. If he ever got into the dating game again, which was a *big* if considering his current mental state, he needed to make sure it was with the right one, that it was the right thing to do.

He wasn't sure, in this case.

Which meant that he needed to keep himself to himself. Focus on getting to the bottom of the haunting on Seafoam Street, and walk away with his data in hand when it came time to return home.

He had no other choice. Work was the most important thing in his life. Marshall intended to keep it that way.

"You were out awfully late."

Marshall nearly jumped out of his skin at the unexpected voice coming from the chair next to his bed. Fumbling ahead and stepping over dirty laundry, he eventually found the light switch and flicked it on.

His uncle didn't even blink.

"Damn, Jack," Marshall muttered, trying to catch his breath, hand pressed to his chest. "Nearly gave me a heart attack."

Jack stared down at his weathered hands, inspecting his fingernails in much the same way a woman would. "And you didn't answer my question."

"I didn't hear a question."

Out came the seal-bark laugh that helped break up some of the tension in the room. Still, Marshall's heart thundered and his lungs pumped overtime to try and get back to normal.

"Even at this time of night, or should I say morning, you're a pretty funny guy, Marshie," Jack stated, shaking his head and rising up out of the chair. "Your mother was worried sick. She's been calling you nonstop since dinner."

Marshall patted his pocket. "I had it on silent. I'm sorry. And I did tell her where I would be last night."

"But not when you'd be home. Which should have been at a decent hour, not…" He waved a hand vaguely in the air.

Marshall huffed. "I'm thirty-two years old. Didn't know I still had a curfew."

"You could have left a note. Mind that you let her know where you're going and when you'll be back. She worries about you."

Jack made it enough of a reprimand to get Marshall's back up. "She worries enough to send you into my room to wait up for me like some kind of guard dog?"

Jack cricked his neck. "Guard dog? No. Came in here with a message for you. Must have dozed off."

"A message?"

"From my girl at the coffee shop. You remember Birdie?" A lustful glint rooted in the old man's eyes.

The weight of exhaustion settled uneasily on his shoulders and Marshall took a moment to lean against the wall, his back aching and his limbs heavy, waiting for Jack to get to the point. With his eyelids drooping and the futon beckoning, he wanted nothing more than to slip under the sheets and embrace the waiting dreamless sleep. Instead, it looked like an early morning heart to heart was in order, but he couldn't for the life of him figure out what Birdie would have to say that was so important his uncle had waited up. "Yeah? And?"

"She wanted me to tell you something about the farmers' market tomorrow."

Marshall bit the inside of his lip. "The…farmers' market," he repeated dully.

"Yeah." Jack scratched the side of his head. "Not sure what she meant by it, but I do know there are quite a few neat little stalls set up. Fruits and veggies too, if you're into that kind of garbage. I'm a steak and potatoes man, myself."

"I'll be sure to make time for the farmers' market." He'd say anything to get his uncle out of the room. "Now, if you don't mind…" Marshall flicked his gaze toward the bed.

"Sure, of course. Shouldn't have fallen asleep in here anyway. Gotta get up in a couple of hours." Jack stepped toward the door, pausing only long enough to clap his nephew on the shoulder. "Kid, welcome to the world of small-town life, where everyone not only knows your business but manages it for you. How are you liking it so far?"

"So far, so good," Marshall conceded on a yawn.

Jack's grip tightened for a second before he released. "Let's see if you'll be saying the same thing in a few days."

The two said their goodnights and Marshall fell into bed moments later, his mind replaying the strange conversation and wondering why an old woman would want him to go to the farmers' market.

———

In the morning, not even the scent of coffee was enough to get him out of his bed before eight. Which counted as sleeping in, in his world. Five hours of sleep was less than his usual but there were things to do and people to meet, apparently, which meant his brain kicked into gear soon after the sun crept between the window blinds.

Marshall spent the majority of his early morning logging the evidence he and Spring had managed to gather the night before, compiling notes and jotting down his observations, entering the data into his laptop.

Not without noting how often Spring's name appeared on the computer document. She'd been a big help to him with his investigation.

He shook his head. There was no sense in denying the

strange attraction he felt for the woman. Strange in that their chemistry, palpable and real, had come out of nowhere despite his efforts to the contrary and after only two days.

He wanted nothing to do with her, didn't he? Why had he managed to cave so easily when it came to working with her?

One kiss had turned him into a simpleton.

"Why are you holed up in here in the dark?"

Marshall started at his mother's question, coming from over his shoulder next to his ear. He hadn't heard her come in.

"I'm working," he replied. Creeping up on him must be a game the brother and sister played, to see who could scare the shit out of Marshall with the slightest provocation.

"You aren't supposed to be working." Emmie walked over to the window and drew open the blinds. "You're supposed to be relaxing and getting out of your own brain."

Marshall winced when bright sunlight filtered into the room, dust motes floating in the air and sparkling like gemstones. "I know I'm not supposed to be working, but in this case, working is fun. I like it. Haven't you heard of pastimes, Mom?"

"You'll like it better once you get out there and meet people your own age. You're still young, Marsh. You need to have some fun. Live a little."

Emmie stood with her hands on her hips, bright golden yellow hair cascading down to her shoulders around a heart-shaped face. Beautiful, yes, but her eyes were all business. Full of loving chastisement for her only son. She'd aged much better than her older brother, who took *haggard* to a whole new level.

Maybe the beach jogging really did do her good.

"I *am* living a little." Marshall leaned back in his chair and studied her. Not ready to give in to the bullying tactics sure to follow. No one could bully quite like a mother with an agenda.

"By studying the dead?" she replied, said with enough tone that her judgment was obvious.

"Okay, you have a point," he groaned. "But I don't want to go out right now. I have to prepare to go back to the Seafoam Street house tonight. I made good progress last night. There were some definitive results that data will support, once I get it plugged into a spreadsheet." He turned his attention back to his laptop.

Emmie crossed the room and pushed him out of his chair with such unexpected strength that Marshall slipped down to the floor. His eyes were wide when his ass hit the floor. "No, you don't. You and I are taking a trip to the farmers' market," she told him.

"Come on, Mom. I don't have time for this. Stop treating me like I'm still a teenager. I'm a grown man." Which instantly brought a flush to his cheeks. If he had to defend himself like this, then he obviously wasn't acting like one.

And again with the farmers' market. What did they sell? Gold bars?

"*You* come on, Marshall. You're only here for a few weeks and I want you to make the most of it. It's bad enough you hole up in your classroom in New York doing God knows what—"

"You mean teaching and shaping young minds?" he put in.

Emmie nudged him with the toe of her little white sneakers. "Get up, Marshall. Put on some sunscreen because you are going to look like a lobster with the tiniest bit of sun, and come with me to the farmers' market. You might enjoy yourself."

He wondered if his uncle had put the idea into Emmie's head or if it was a strange coincidence. Either way, he had little choice but to do as directed. Marshall considered himself a mildly intelligent individual. Which meant he knew better than to cross his mother.

Forty minutes later he had a basket over one arm and

three bags slung on the other. Emmie's personal shopping assistant. Not only did his muscles ache, but his cheeks were on fire from perpetual smiling. His mother knew almost everyone she encountered and had to stop at each stall to say something to the person manning it. It was enough to make him wish he'd stayed in bed that morning.

He resigned himself to a terrible morning of endless conversation and vegetables, until something smacked into the back of his head.

Marshall whirled around, his glasses askew.

"Oops, sorry!"

The sweetly familiar tone twined around his heart and constricted faster than an anaconda with its next meal. Spring Astin.

And yes, she looked ready to eat him.

It was almost enough to have him forgiving that she'd launched an apple at his head, quite on purpose. "What are you doing here?" he asked, adjusting the bags and moving closer to her booth.

"Taking a little time off to enjoy the finer things in life." She balanced another perfect red apple in one palm. "My boss gave me the weekend off from paperwork but this was her trade."

Marshall glanced around him at the throngs of people. "This is fun for you?"

"Oh, sure. Look at the decorations! Squash and gourds and apples everywhere, pumpkins ready to be carved into jack-o-lanterns, cornstalks and hay bales. Not to mention I get a sneak preview of the kids in their costumes."

Indeed, the longer Marshall stared at the crowd, the more he noticed children prancing between their parents, dressed in ghoulish getup and face paint. About a week too early in his opinion. They had another twelve days before Halloween.

He felt the scowl melt away as he turned back to see Spring's smile. A smile like that could be infectious.

"I suppose it's pretty nice," he grumbled. "Everyone seems to be in a wonderful mood."

Emmie stopped by to place another bag over Marshall's arm and give Spring a once-over from top to toe. Mom-style. Seeing everything and more in that look even when it lasted less than five seconds. Spring held up under the pressure like a champ. If anything, she shone brighter.

"Marshall." Emmie's face broke into a reserved grin. "You didn't introduce me to your friend."

"I thought you knew everyone in town already," he responded lightly. "Emmie Rownan, meet Spring Astin." He decided that honesty was the best policy for all involved, but the kiss he'd keep to himself. "She's going to be helping me with the old Seafoam House investigation while I'm in town."

"Another ghost hunter!" Emmie said it with such insincere sweetness that only Marshall recognized the way she shivered. His mother didn't like anything to do with the paranormal. She frightened too easily. "I don't know how you guys can stand it. Don't places like that give you the creeps?"

With barely contained energy Spring reached out to shake the woman's hand. "Just kind of a passion of mine, although there are a few truly creepy moments involved. That's what makes life special! Besides, I deal with much scarier situations on a day to day basis."

"Oh? What is it that you do, dear?"

"I'm a camp counselor."

Emmie set her lips in a thin smile. "Yes, I imagine you definitely do have some terrifying situations in that field. I'm just glad I only had one little hellion to deal with." She bumped Marshall to let him know she spoke of him, as though it hadn't been obvious.

The two ladies chatted for another moment before Emmie headed off to the next booth with a wave over her shoulder. "She's on a mission," Marshall told Spring. "She wants to see how many people she can talk to in one day. I think she's on track to set a record."

"Tell that to the Golden Girls there," Spring replied with a chuckle and a nod to the trio of older ladies manning the next booth over, chatting up a storm with anyone and everyone who strolled by. "They love a challenge."

The mention of the three matchmakers—how could they be anything but, now that he recognized their sly attempt to get him out and about—had goose bumps breaking out over Marshall's skin despite the heat. "Hey, do you want to get out of here? I mean, do you have time?" he hurried to ask. "I could use a little fresh air away from so many people."

"You're getting a little anxious, eh?"

"You could say that."

"And here I thought you New Yorkers were used to crowds." One shoulder raised in a semi-shrug, and the sunny yellow fabric of her shirt slipped lower to reveal more golden tanned skin. His mouth went dry.

"I...I don't get out much."

"Well, it depends on what you have in mind," Spring stated, her eyes dancing over his.

"I don't know. I thought it might be good to take in some scenery. We can walk on the beach and you can tell me about the native wildlife."

"Is *walk on the beach* code for something else, Professor?"

"It's entirely what you make of it. I will, however, promise to be a perfect gentleman the entire time," he told her.

There must have been something in his tone that belied the statement, for Spring's face broke out in a dazzling smile. "I knew you couldn't get enough of me. You can set your bags under the table. Coraline will watch them and make sure they're still there when your mom comes back to grab 'em. Cora! Brinley!"

Spring called out to the two girls manning a table along-side her and informed them she was taking a break. They couldn't have been more than eighteen, long black hair and sweeping eyelashes coupled with skin-tight clothing. Neither one said a word when Spring stashed Marshall's bags beneath the table and fell into step beside him.

"I work with those two at the camp," she told him in a conspirator's whisper as they walked away. "They have no clue what they're doing half the time but they are great with kids. Especially prepubescent boys." She gave him a wink. "And sometimes we sell whatever arts and crafts the campers make at the farmers' market, then put the money back into the camp."

"That's actually a great idea," he agreed.

"It benefits us all around. One of the many new systems implemented by my bestie when she came on board last year." Spring nudged Marshall with her elbow. "You know, the day before you came to town I coaxed her into the old Seafoam House."

His ears perked up. "Did you give her a personal ghost tour?"

Spring's forceful exhalation ruffled her bangs. "I tried to. She was so scared she had *me* jumping at every little noise. And I'm not one to jump easily. Around midnight she couldn't take it anymore, so we left. But not before I saw a shadow in the upstairs hallway."

Marshall paused long enough for Spring to kick off her sandals, looping the straps around her wrist before they moved across the sand. His sneakers sank in deep but he could feel the heat coming off the sand. He'd stick with the sneakers until they made it closer to the water.

"So you've experienced phenomena in that house before. I was hoping last night went well for you. I mean, I hope you weren't too rattled by the findings," he amended.

Spring stared at him with one eyebrow raised. "Are you kidding me? Last night was amazing. It was like a dream come true. We're going back again tonight, right?"

"Not tonight. Monday night, if it's not too much trouble for you."

"No, I'll be fine. I've always been gifted with excess energy. Most of the time, at least. It helps me run after the campers on very little caffeine and ensures I don't need much sleep at night. I'm all yours!"

All his? That was what he was afraid of.

"Hey, you wanted to know about local wildlife, right?" Spring tugged on his t-shirt and pointed toward the surf. "There's Dave."

"What's special about Dave?"

"He's a town original who never talks to anyone. He just walks along the beach collecting trash." Spring nudged him with her shoulder. "Go on, try to get him to talk. Say something to him."

"But you said he never talks to anyone."

"I know. I'm proving my point. Go on."

With one last glance toward Spring, Marshall reluctantly raised his arm. "Hey there, Dave! How you doing, man?" he called out.

The rail-thin fellow kept his head down and his attention focused on the sand in front of him, long-legged strides eating up the beach as he moved away. He said nothing and never once looked over.

Marshall turned to see Spring bent over in a fit of laughter. "This is the strangest place I've ever been to," he mumbled.

"Professor, we are just getting started. Now walk with me and tell me more about your life."

She laced her arm through his. And Marshall wondered if he'd begun to dig his own grave where Spring was concerned.

CHAPTER SEVEN

*S*pring stood in front of a mirror, scrutinizing how her hair twisted around her face in loose curls. Partly from the humidity, partly from her own effort in an attempt to put on a pretty face without going overboard. Already she'd washed off makeup three times trying to get the perfect natural look and failing each time.

"Why don't you forgo makeup altogether?" Mecca asked, lounging on Spring's bed. She kicked her feet up in the air, lying flat on her stomach. "I mean, you're a beautiful woman, radiant no matter where you are. That house is dark and disgusting. You don't need to try this hard to catch his attention."

Spring pinched her cheeks. "Who said I'm trying hard?"

"I know you. I've seen you get ready for a date. *Multiple* dates, from Tradewinds to Shenanigans to the back of a pickup truck filled with blankets. Which has been my personal favorite of your dates, might I add." Mecca swung her legs around to the side of the bed and shifted her position. "Why are you so concerned with this one?"

"Because this isn't a *date*," Spring replied hotly. She fixed herself with a look to remind her not to go overboard, then puckered her lips. "This is a strange situation where we both know how much we want each other, but he's playing hard to get. I can tell he's curious about me but he...oh, I don't know. He's scared or something."

Think of it. A man playing hard to get. Or at least pretending he didn't feel things that he almost certainly did.

If Spring didn't know better, she'd say her sexy professor was nothing more than a beautiful idiot when it came to women.

"Is it really playing hard to get when someone tells you they don't want a relationship?" Mecca posited.

"Yes. No." Spring sighed. "I don't know." In reality, she didn't know. Not really. She had theories concerning Marshall's strange hot and cold behavior, but without actively sitting down to talk to him about it, her theories only got her so far. And it was a conversation best held in person after at least a couple more days of getting to know each other.

Spring had learned the hard way that if she took a dive off that long board into the deep end of a pool too soon, she usually ended up swimming alone. Or busting her head before struggling to come up for air.

Which was fine. No, really, it was. A lot of guys couldn't handle her intensity right up front, and she'd gotten used to letting them drift away and going on with her life. With Marshall, she didn't want to push him too far too fast. Yet sadly they were on a deadline. He'd said he was only in town for two weeks. Which meant that Spring had less than ten days to convince him that she was the right woman for him.

His feelings are like a glass coffin: remains to be seen.

"Just don't do what you normally do," Mecca replied easily as Spring continued to make strange faces at herself in the mirror.

"What is it I normally do?"

"You throw yourself at a man without seeing the full picture."

"Sometimes throwing myself is fun. I regret nothing."

"Good, I'm glad to hear it. But from what you've told me —shockingly little in comparison to your usual novels of information—it seems like you're serious about this guy."

Spring whirled around, a wand of lip gloss raised halfway to her lips. Bright red. *Was* she going overboard? "What if I am?"

Mecca blinked. "Nothing wrong with it. I don't want you to get hurt is all. It's bad enough you insist on hanging out in a haunted house—"

"A really cool, awesome haunted house," Spring clarified.

"Yeah, I feel like you're more likely to break your leg than break your heart," Mecca grumbled.

"Trust me that I know what I'm doing. I like this guy, sure, and I think we can have a lot of fun together. But soon he'll be leaving and going back to New York. Without starting a relationship with me." Unless she managed to flip the script.

"Somehow I get the feeling you want to change his mind."

Spring shrugged. "If he *happens* to change his mind, then I won't stop him."

She finished primping and decided to go with practical skinny jeans and a dark t-shirt. Sneakers completed the ensemble, and she pulled up to the Seafoam Street house with Mecca's parting logic rattling around inside her brain:

Don't do anything stupid.

Um, how long had they been friends? *Of course* Spring planned on doing something stupid. Tonight, that included seducing Marshall Rownan.

Too soon? Probably. Her mother the psychologist would have a field day with Spring's head if she knew how quickly her only daughter jumped into and out of relationships with boyfriends.

But Spring had never been one to be careful with her heart. She believed firmly in living for the moment. She figured she'd only get one shot at true love, even if that meant trying and trying again until she found The One. And so she made her trying count regardless of the potential for pain.

Or heartbreak, as Mecca pointed out.

Boundaries came later, once she'd gotten whatever wild hairs out of her system. She had a sneaking suspicion that Marshall would prove to be more than a simple one-nighter, at least once he got over his confusion regarding her.

Tonight, he waited for her on the porch of Seafoam House as she parked the car.

The smile on her face quickly melted away at seeing the look on his face. Dark, angry, brows drawn together and fists clenched at his sides. "Hey there. What's the matter?" she asked, worried.

"Bad news," he barked out, stalking toward the front door and pushing it open.

"Uh-oh. Your body language tells me something happened."

"Yeah, your little back window entrance?" His shoulders hunched forward, shaking. "Seems you aren't the only one who knew about it."

Her heart sank down through her chest and landed low in her gut. "Someone broke the glass?"

"Not just that. They stole my laptop. Took some of the larger pieces of equipment but trashed the rest."

Spring hurried up the porch steps and into the living room behind him. The stench of mildew hit her and she pushed it aside, gaze sweeping the mess in front of her. She was used to the grime and decay. She didn't expect to see the table overturned and pieces of loose wire and plastic strewn across the floor.

Who could have done such a thing?

"I don't understand," she began slowly. Trying to put the pieces together in her mind.

Marshall stepped up behind her, his hand pushing rigid

strokes through his blond hair. "I'm not sure what happened. I locked the window—"

"Yeah, don't I know it."

"But someone broke the glass and came in anyway. I thought you said this place was safe!" he exploded. "That this kind of thing doesn't happen here!"

"I mean, what place is *really* safe?" Spring argued. She nudged a broken bit of unidentifiable plastic with her foot. "I never thought something like this would happen in Cinnamon Bay. We've had our fair share of kids with cans of spray paint, but nothing on this magnitude. I'm so sorry, Marshall."

He stalked to the staircase and sank down on the bottom step, burying his head in his hands. "So am I. That equipment wasn't cheap. This is devastating."

She hated the way he spoke. Defeated. Mentally drained. "I mean, I can give you some money to put toward it."

"What?" He shook his head at her. "No, absolutely not. This wasn't your fault."

Why did it feel like it fell on her shoulders, then? "I don't know what to say," she whispered, kneeling to start gathering bits of broken equipment and feeling like she was also gathering broken pieces of her heart.

Someone had come here, had forced their way inside, and done something unthinkable. Something that impacted not only Marshall but her as well. Whoever it was had a lot of nerve and too much time on their hands.

This didn't feel like mere vandals, or neighborhood kids doing mischief. Was it personal?

"Say nothing, unless you have a good joke for me. I could really use a laugh right now," Marshall stated on an exhale. "I mean, this is crazy. Isn't it? We finally get a few quantifiable results and someone does this to us? I think... No." He broke off, shaking his head to clear whatever thought had popped up.

She shifted to crouch next to him and used her hands to push the rubbish into a center pile. "I hope you have insurance."

"*That's* your idea of a joke?"

"No," she said and swallowed a laugh. "It was a legitimate question. I want to know if you have insurance or if I need to give you some cash. I feel responsible."

Marshall stared at her, his gaze penetrating. Searching for answers neither one of them appeared to have. "You're *not* responsible, okay?" he said slowly. "This isn't even vandalism. It's too focused. This is on me. There are people...well, never mind that. But if this place was accessible to the public for years via your secret entrance and this never happened before, then it must have something to do with me. Don't worry about it."

Spring sighed. "I know you're trying to make me feel better but please stop getting down on yourself. We have work to do and I don't want you to feel defeated before we've even truly begun."

"But we got our best results that first night—"

"Our best results *so far*," she corrected.

"Still, all that data was on the laptop, which is gone. How can we prove our findings without it?"

"You still have your handwritten notes, right? You wrote everything down in that notebook."

"Which is back at my mother's place. Yes, I suppose the data could be re-entered, but that would take time."

She shrugged. "It will be worth the investment in time. I'll help."

He shook his head, apparently finding more excuses. "But we still need to back it up with verifiable data from instruments, otherwise we could have just made it all up. Which means starting from scratch with proper equipment. Spring, we can't work without equipment." His tone told her it was hopeless and she was being a fool to think otherwise.

Too bad he didn't know her well. Yet. "Not a problem. I know a couple of people with video cameras that we can borrow. Maybe even some super-sensitive temperature gauges to track cold spots. A simple digital voice recorder can catch EVPs, yes? With a little bit of good old-fashioned ingenuity, we can make this work!"

Marshall watched her scuttle around the living room gathering the broken gadgets in her arms, and his chuckle shocked her into stillness. A first for her. "You are something else, Miss Astin."

She paused long enough to give him a wink, shaking her rump a little before resuming her cleanup efforts. "And you will never find another like me."

Better he knew it up front.

They put in a good two hours of time cleaning up, salvaging what could be salvaged, and creating a list of equipment that would either need to be fixed or replaced. Through it all, Spring felt the heavy weight of eyes on her, and this time she wasn't sure if it was ghosts or something—*someone*—else.

She also wasn't sure which proposition scared her more: the living or the dead. Ghosts didn't destroy the equipment, of that she was certain.

"I think we need to take a break for a minute."

She glanced up in time to see Marshall swinging his bag over his shoulder, his gaze capturing hers. "You can take a break if you need one. I still have too much work to do," he replied.

Spring propped her fists on her hips and speared him with a look. "If your mood doesn't improve, then this is going to be a long unproductive night. And until we get the equipment we need back up and running, there's really not much we can do anyway. Your words."

Marshall pursed his lips in thought, his mind a million miles away. She never expected him to say, "I heard Shenanigans is having a two-for-one drink special."

It took a moment for his words to kick in past the automatic defenses in her brain. Was Marshall asking her out on a date? She briefly considered clarifying it with him—in a teasing way, of course—and in the end, bit her tongue. "They do have some really killer drinks," she replied sweetly. "They also have extended hours with Halloween coming up. You're actually going to listen to me for once, Professor?"

"It *is* my vacation," he grumbled, stalking over to the card table they'd set up again. He slammed his bag down. "I never really drink. It might be fun."

So maybe not an honest to goodness date. But a start, at least. Spring jumped up, looping her arm through his despite his startled expression. "Then let's do it! I'm willing to bet that I can drink you under the table in an hour flat."

"You seriously want to challenge me," Marshall said, shaking his head.

"Yes, I seriously do want to challenge you. There also happens to be a food challenge at Shenanigans. You know they have pub grub? Well, apparently there is a fried mozzarella sticks platter weighing twenty pounds. If two people can finish that and a pitcher of beer or soda in fifteen minutes, they get their meal free!"

He grimaced. "That sounds disgusting. You're on."

Together, they carried the broken equipment out to his car, locking the door behind them. Spring surprised him further by jumping in his front passenger seat instead of taking her own car. The key slid in the ignition and he pulled away from the curb, leaving the hulking skeleton of Seafoam House behind them, its windows dark and unforgiving.

A tiny shiver ran down her spine and Spring made sure to keep her focus ahead. "The winners get free t-shirts too. It's kind of a big thing. Picture on the *wall* kind of big."

"And how many pictures are currently on the wall?"

"About twelve."

Marshall pressed his foot down on the gas. "Then let's make it thirteen."

***

_W_ith the platter in front of them, Spring wished she would have goaded him into something else. Something that would not require her to undo the top button on her jeans and show how she could _really_ put away food.

Unfortunately, she'd been the one to suggest the mozzarella sticks eating challenge and here they were, with fifteen minutes to finish twenty pounds.

Maybe Marshall was right. Maybe it was disgusting, and had potential for turning into something gross as well.

What had she been thinking?

This was not the kind of thing to do on a first date when you wanted to impress someone. Even if it wasn't technically a date. Now they'd either both end up with stomachaches—pretty much a given—or he'd think her repulsive and definitely not date-worthy.

Marshall's eyes had gone wide and he stared at the loaded platter of deep-fried cheese. Already green around the gills? But that could be the overhead lighting. She hoped.

"Why did I let you talk me into this?" he moaned, completely ignoring the cheering crowd around them.

Spring wondered the same thing but wisely kept a smile plastered on her face. "Are you ready?"

"No. I will never be ready."

The buzzer dinged and the wait staff yelled to signal the start of their time. With a final grin at her "date's" face, Spring dug in with a zest she usually reserved for men or food.

This time, she had both in front of her.

They didn't end up winning t-shirts, she lamented later as

they strolled down the boardwalk, but they'd had fun. Wasn't for lack of trying. They'd simply run out of time. But it took their minds off of the break-in at the Seafoam Street house for a while.

"I never want to look at another cheese stick again in my life." Marshall patted his stomach. "Look at me. I'm waddling like a duck. How can they seriously expect two people to handle that much cheese? It's blasphemous!"

Spring chuckled, although she found it difficult to walk herself. Her balance was skewed by the solid weight in her stomach. "Come on, admit it. You had fun." She placed a hand over her mouth to keep the burp inside where it belonged.

"Oh, I won't tell you that I didn't," Marshall stated. "I've never partaken in an eating challenge before. But I don't think I'll need to eat for the next week. It might also adversely affect my desire for all dairy products in the future."

"Heaven forbid! We wouldn't want you to miss out on the dairy treats of the world. What have I done?" She flung her hands up to her cheeks in an exaggerated horrified gesture.

"How could you, woman? I will never want to eat ice cream again because of this."

She glanced over her shoulder to where the ice cream shop sat locked for the night. Ready for another full day of business in the morning. "Yeah, too bad for you they are already closed. Otherwise, I'd get a cone and eat it in front of you just to make you miserable."

It would make her miserable, too, but she couldn't resist the joke.

Marshall's eyes bugged out of his head. "If you can actually fit anything else in your body right now, then I will be in awe of you. You are too tiny to put anything else in there."

She smiled at the idea of him being in awe of her. It was easy to be with him, she thought. Too easy. Spring wondered at the lightness in her heart. The way everything seemed to go still and steady when Marshall stood next to her.

Did he feel the same way?

They headed down a small set of stairs toward the sand and took off their shoes. Rather, Marshall took off his shoes, unlacing them and setting them neatly aside where no one would bother them. Spring kicked her sandals off and let them stay wherever they landed. Not that anyone was around to see. The cell phone in her pocket told her it was after ten and the beach around them, illuminated by the moon overhead, was blissfully empty.

"This is the second time in as many days that we've ended up on this beach," Marshall commented. "Seems all we do is walk."

"And we're significantly more bloated this time around."

His laugh made her heart turn over. "*Significantly*."

The sand cool beneath her feet, Spring raced as best she could toward the ocean, the breeze wild in her hair and trailing along her arms like a lover. She inhaled deeply, taking that wildness inside of her. Making it a part of her.

"I can't believe you've never done an eating contest like that before. Everyone should try something like that at least once in their life. What do you do for fun?" she called out, turning around and walking backwards so she could watch him.

"I do what anyone else does." Marshall carefully picked his way toward the surf. "I work, I go home. Sleep. In the morning, I do it again."

"And in your free time?"

He rubbed at his eyes, and when he lowered his hands, a smile graced his face. "Ah, there's your big mistake. Thinking that I actually have free time to spare."

"You obviously do, if you investigate haunted houses as a pastime."

Those hands went back to his head to push strands of

windblown hair away from his face. "That was something an ex got me into. I'd thought it a joke before then. Someone's way of scaring other people or trying to make a buck. But she convinced me to give it a chance. I did."

They fell into step together on the sand. "What changed your mind?" Spring asked, trying to ignore the hot flame of jealousy igniting beneath her collar bone. She didn't want to think about Marshall with anyone else, no matter how many times she told herself to tread lightly.

Mine, her inner cavewoman growled, baring her teeth.

"I'd like to tell you that I had a *come to Jesus* moment, as my mother might say," Marshall continued. He stopped in front of Spring and together the two of them kicked their way through the surf. "A time when everything fell into place and maybe there was a ghostly hand on my shoulder... Truth is I found a way to connect my love of engineering with the mystery of paranormal phenomena. I married the two, you could say."

"You're going into professor mode." The observation came quickly and burst into being before she could think of something better to say. Something wittier that would keep him talking.

"Ah, it happens. I'm sorry. Anyway, I realized that I'd judged an entire field prematurely. The personal relationship fell through, but my hobbies expanded to include ghost hunting. It seems silly when I think about it—"

"Not at all," she interrupted. "I think it's nice that you gave something outside of your comfort zone a chance. It shows a real willingness to embrace life."

"I think the mozzarella sticks have gone to your head." Marshall stopped again, his fingertips going to her temples and probing her skull. For what, she didn't know. "You're going esoteric on me."

"I'm following your lead. I like a man who knows when to go for it, when to give things a chance, things that he might not ordinarily have found appealing." Her eyes half-closed when he continued to stare at her, continued to massage her temples.

Was she still talking about ghost hunting? No, and Marshall knew it as well. He stared at her with a gaze that saw past the comment. A gaze that saw everything she wanted him to see.

"What am I doing?" he asked slowly.

The question didn't seem to be directed at her. Spring, however, decided to take the initiative.

She covered his hands with her own. "I think you're taking a chance on something." Call it the moonlight making her feel things. Call it emotions swinging up where they had no business being. But the whole of her drew toward him, something inside opening up to envelop him. To claim him.

"You might be right." His voice dropped low. "This is a terrible idea."

It didn't stop her from leaning closer, even as his words turned into a cold chill on the back of her neck. "Why so negative?"

"Not negative. *Realistic*. There's a difference between the two. I already told you that I didn't want to get into anything while I'm visiting, least of all a relationship. Plus I'm not sure if this is right, and that would be the only thing to convince me to make the leap. If it's *right*. You and I think very differently on a number of things—"

"Marshall?" she interrupted.

He blinked at her. "What?"

"Stop talking and kiss me."

The command did the trick and it was Marshall who closed the distance between them. Marshall who fastened his lips on hers and let the rest of the world dissolve. Marshall who gave in to the temptation to at last follow her down this path. To make that leap when anyone else might have chosen to play it safe.

What did those people know about living?

"I love your mouth," he managed to say, their bodies slowly moving closer until their entire fronts were pressed together. "I want to do all kinds of things to your mouth." His fingers curled in her hair to keep her from breaking away.

Spring groaned her agreement. "No one is stopping you."

Her arms wound around his neck, held tight as though he might run away at any moment. When his lips found hers a second time, she gave in to the sensation of falling. It was like the ground dropped out from under her feet and she plummeted. Farther and farther down until the only thing keeping her anchored was Marshall.

He'd probably hate knowing that. He'd hate knowing how she really felt about him, because Spring was definitely one of those people who jumped first and considered the consequences much, much later. If at all.

If she stopped to consider the consequences of falling for Marshall, she might never resurface. The swell would be too big. The changes too much to handle.

Her stomach tied itself into knots again and again. Her blood raced, pulse thumping in her ears, and with the moon so bright and the surf crashing, Spring knew she'd stepped into her own private fairy tale.

At least until Marshall broke them apart. "This is a bad idea," he repeated, his breathing shallow.

She smacked him on the chest. Her lips felt swollen. "Can you cut it out with the bad idea bit?"

"I'm saying that if we spend tonight together, you and me, then I won't be content with one night. I'll want more. I want more than one night with you, Spring."

He said it as though tonight was all they'd get and he hated the idea.

That thrilled her. "Who's to say what will and won't happen? It pays to live in the moment, Professor, because in the end that's all we've got. Make the most of each second. If you want to go to bed with me," her lashes fluttered closed, "then nothing should stop you."

"Oh, so you'd like me to throw you over my shoulder and drag you back to my mother's house to ravage you in her guest bedroom?" Marshall retorted hotly.

His mother's house? That definitely wouldn't do.

"No. But if you're serious, then I live just down the road. Alone." Spring hiked a thumb over her shoulder in what she hoped was the direction of her house. "We have all night. I'd like to spend it with you. If those mozzarella sticks didn't do permanent damage to your insides, that is."

One eyebrow rose independently of the other. "Once again it sounds as though you are challenging me."

"Once again you'd be *correct*, sir."

He reached for her hand, pulling her toward the board-walk where they'd left their shoes. "Come on. Before I change my mind."

It wasn't the most romantic invitation she'd ever had, but Spring smiled regardless. Her heart melted a little more when his fingers linked through hers.

She'd convince him, surely, that one night would never be enough for them.

CHAPTER EIGHT

Marshall decided he'd had quite enough walking for the night. Especially with his stomach full and his blood pumping toward his lower extremities. He pulled his car into Spring's driveway, following her directions carefully and driving slowly to avoid any nighttime road hazards. The pitcher of beer they'd shared had worked out of their systems during their walk, thank goodness, but he wanted to make sure he didn't leave anything to chance.

The slightest hiccup and he'd take it as a sign to follow his head rather than the southern parts of his anatomy.

His head still told him that he wasn't sure if things were right, bedding this wild woman. Despite how he desperately wanted her. The rest of him told his head to shut up.

He went with the latter.

They made it to her front porch before Spring had her hands fisted in his shirt, dragging him toward where she stood one riser higher on the steps. Using the leverage to her advantage.

"I don't want you to leave," she murmured against his throat.

He chuckled, shifting to nip at her ear. "Trust me. I'm not

going anywhere." He'd made up his mind. Or rather, he'd acquiesced to his loins. He still had no clue if this was the right move, but he planned on going for it.

And here he stood, his legs straightened, knees locking to keep him in place and upright.

"I don't mean tonight. I mean going back to New York."

"Oh." Marshall paused, then continued his ministrations, laving the side of her neck with his tongue. "I wish I didn't have to go so soon."

"You don't," she insisted. "You can stay here with me." She meant it as a joke. Only she wasn't joking, and Spring instantly regretted putting the idea out in the open.

"If I had any sense, I would run away from you. Far away. You're lethal," he replied gruffly.

She pointed to her chest. "It isn't my fault!"

"You have this way about you. This way of making me do things I don't want to do."

She recognized the hint of reluctance in his voice. "You mean," she began, her dark eyes searching his face, "you don't want to kiss me? I thought you liked my mouth. I thought you wanted to do all kinds of things to my mouth."

He joined her on the same step, his fingers feathering over her chin, down her neck. "I do. And I don't."

"What do you want to do then, Marshall?" Her heart pounded the closer he got to her. The longer he touched her.

When he bent his head to hers, his eyes burning with desire, with hunger, she wanted to fall to her knees. "I'll do whatever I can for you. Give you whatever I can tonight. Because you deserve it."

She raised her arms to his shoulders automatically. Tightening her hold and leaning closer at the edge of resolve creeping into his voice. "Not tomorrow?" she questioned.

Marshall's response was to swing her up into his arms, walking up the rest of the steps to her front porch and using his elbow to nudge the door open. The door she'd left unlocked, he thought briefly. He'd have to remind her of the dangers come morning.

"Give yourself to me tonight, Spring," he said softly. "We can start there."

His mouth took hers in clear demand. The heat of him tempted her. Enticed her. His touch melted away whatever sane thoughts were left until there was nothing except Marshall. Spring didn't realize when he'd brought her up to her second-floor bedroom. Or the fact that his arms were shaking, his lungs pumping, and his eyes blazing when he dropped her on the bed. She saw nothing except his strong shoulders when he pulled his shirt over his head, keeping eye contact with her.

There was his amazing mouth when he lowered down to her, his arms a cage around her. His mesmerizing voice when he told her how beautiful she looked.

"I can't promise you tomorrow," Marshall murmured between kisses, pressing his chest to hers and forcing her back toward her pillows. "But I'll give you whatever you want tonight. Don't you feel it?" He grabbed her hand and brought it to his chest. "I'm hungry for you. I want you more than anything, and tonight I won't give you up."

"Don't give me up ever," she said on a sigh. "Trust your heart, Marshall."

He silenced her with another kiss, and she felt her body begin to tremble under the weight of her feelings. Feelings she hadn't wanted, expected, or needed until she met him.

Her back was against her headboard with Marshall crowding her front. Fire raced along her skin where he touched her, his bare chest tempting her. His fingers gripped her wrists and brought her arms above her head.

There was a curious wrenching in her heart when he stared down at her. "Hush," he told her, his voice dark. "No more talking."

Her tongue darted out to wet her lower lip, pulse racing in

her ears. With his hands gentling on her, his eyes hungry and burning, she didn't remember how to breathe. She didn't remember a time when there wasn't Marshall. How could she go back to being alone when he left?

There was no mistaking it: he would be leaving. Leaving her behind.

She pushed the knowledge aside and drew in a breath. She could do this. There was nothing in her past that hadn't prepared her. Her hands framed his face and she brought him down to meet her. The tips of his fingers brushed at the hem of her top, and her body went still. Marshall pulled her shirt over her head in one movement. It left her exposed to him.

He spent a good minute attending to her lacy bra, nuzzling her nipples through the material before reaching for the clasp. Then he bent his head low and flicked his tongue across her skin. Spring closed her eyes as he lapped at her, nibbling, suckling. It was a new level of sensuality. One she'd never experienced with any man before.

He took great care to ready her, shedding her clothing as he did everything else—with single-minded tenacity. His body moved hot and aggressive against hers as he bent his attention to her hips. Her ribs. She hadn't thought it sexy when a man paid attention to those zones before. But Marshall brought a new intensity to the experience.

His hand spanned her stomach, his lips on her throat. "Give yourself to me tonight, Spring."

Tonight. And forever. She knew it even when he did not. They'd found each other through time and space. Across lifetimes.

She cried out for him when he moved away, kicking off his jeans and exposing his erection for the first time. Her gaze was riveted, taking in his pale skin. The muscles she hadn't expected.

Then she squealed when he lifted her into his arms. "The shower." He held her against him, moving into the bathroom.

Spring latched her legs around his hips, his hard length bouncing against her rear with each step. "You want to have sex in the shower?" She gasped when he brought both of them right in and turned the water on. "*In cold water?*" It was more a scream than a statement.

It warmed quickly, raining down on them as he aggressively backed her against the tile wall. He dipped his mouth to hers and she gasped, curling her fingers around his arms and holding onto him when she couldn't quite catch her balance. Spring lifted her leg around him, bringing her core into contact with his arousal.

It was different, she thought when he fastened his mouth to hers, tongue sweeping through her closed lips. This kind of need was different. Fierce, in direct contrast to his usual quiet demeanor.

They moved under the steamy sweep of water, his hands sliding possessively over her skin, down past her hips in slow and deliberate movements. *Good.* He needed to take his time. To memorize every inch of her so that he could miss her when he left.

His mouth never stopped, his kisses like drugs. With the hot water rushing down her back, it urged her closer, her hands clutching his neck and hair as a firestorm of need raged through her.

His hands moved to cup her breasts, thumbs tweaking her nipples before sliding down her ribs to find the sensitive area hidden in the triangle of curls between her legs. There was electricity in his touch, and he left trails of lightning along her skin. God, she needed...*needed*... He kept her on the edge until she wanted to scream and beg for relief.

"Please," she moaned, thrusting her chest up at him. There was a sound bubbling up inside of her, a cross between a purr and a plea. It did something to him. Marshall's mouth left hers and kissed a trail of fire down to the tip of her breast.

"Is this what you want?"

Spring cried out when he took her nipple between his teeth, nibbling slightly. She arched up into him, reaching out to grab his erection. If she didn't touch him she would burst. Which wouldn't necessarily be a bad thing. But she'd be in a billion pieces and unable to watch him move toward completion. Then his fingers found her, his mouth tugging strongly, both teasing her in tandem. His knee nudged her legs apart. Between the pounding water and the intense pressure, she was toast.

The sane part of her realized it was happening too fast. They'd only known each other for five days. Five beautiful days where she dreamed of his face, his eyes burning into her. Was it love? She couldn't be sure.

"Are you ready for me?" he asked, pushing wet hair out of his eyes.

"Don't you think we should…" Spring wasn't on birth control. She needed to be safe, not stupid, especially since they were rushing things.

"You're right. Yeah, you're right." On a groan, he kissed her roughly and bolted out of the shower.

Spring paused under the water while she waited for him, a flush causing her skin to be ultra-sensitive. She chuckled softly, leaning back until her head knocked against the wall. What was she doing? Going out of her damn mind, apparently. Normally it wouldn't matter. She'd been known to indulge in a one-night stand or two in her life. But this was different.

It was different with Marshall.

He hurried back into the shower, with a condom already rolled down over his erection.

"There you are," she said, beckoning him forward with the crook of a finger and a sly grin.

Marshall was like a bull running toward a red flag. He pressed against her, thick. Lusty.

Trapped between his body and the wall, Spring couldn't move. She didn't want to. His teeth scraped against the side of her neck in an enticement that made her want to wrap herself around him. Giving in to temptation, she jumped, knowing he would catch her, and her legs wrapped around his waist.

"Are you ready for *me*, now?" she asked in a repeat of his earlier words.

"Born ready."

And Marshall thrust deep as though he had every right to take possession. He buried himself inside her to the hilt with a thoroughly masculine growl.

It was ecstasy. He slipped out of her only to thrust home again and again, thick and heavy. There was no holding back. She surrendered herself to him completely, her fingernails tracing patterns on his back, her whispered pleas begging for more. She wanted this more than anything, more than she wanted to see tomorrow.

His body moved with hers, faster and harder. Spring trembled and felt like she was shaking apart, fragmenting. Only his arms held her in place when she would have melted. She clenched around him, ready for release, tightening in demand and urging him on. He continued mindlessly, their bodies dancing together until his rhythm increased.

Soon they fell over the edge of orgasm together.

CHAPTER NINE

Spring opened her eyes drowsily. Sexily, Marshall thought, since he'd been staring at her for the last ten minutes. He smiled and reached over to touch her lightly swollen lower lip. He might have gone a little too hard. Especially considering he'd had her twice more after their shower together. The last time, he'd kept their bodies locked together, staying inside her for as long as possible, unwilling to break the connection.

Wow, he'd missed this. Not just the sex, although it had been a long time since he'd partaken in those types of extracurricular activities. He missed the conversation and the laughter and the cuddles that followed. Knew full well those intimacies didn't happen often.

Spring's smile was lazy and satisfied. "What are you thinking about?" she prompted.

Marshall shifted as close as possible. "I'm thinking how crazy you make me feel. I've never done this before."

"What, you're telling me you've never had sex with a woman before? I don't believe you," she teased, propping her chin on her hand.

"Never jumped into bed with a woman I hardly know. It's not my style. And I hardly know you at all, yet I feel like that isn't important. Because I want more than your body. I appreciate your mind. Your character." His touch gentled as he tracked a thumb from her chin down her neck to the hollow. "You are so different from me."

"You're saying all the right things." She sighed, pushing her hair out of her face until it hung loosely over her shoulders. Like a siren, Marshall thought. She'd certainly drawn him in, with a lure he hadn't been able to resist. "Too bad we both know you're leaving," she finished at last.

With a sigh of his own, he drew his fingers down her arm. "There are a whole lot of other issues you don't know about. Things I don't particularly care to get into right now. Things about my life that aren't in order."

She shifted, and Marshall automatically twined their legs together. It was ease, it was comfort. Way too damn comfortable right off the bat. That kind of feeling could lead to complacency, and that's when people showed their true colors. He didn't want to think about true colors, or people showing a single side of themselves and waiting for the right moment to let the rest of them come through. The right moment could be weeks, months, years in the making. He didn't have time for any of it.

He'd make time, one day, when the timing and the person were right. He told himself as much repeatedly, even when his inner voice urged him to look at Spring and reconsider.

"Ah, so it's an ex-lover issue," she said to clarify.

She cut right to the chase, of course. Marshall expected nothing less of her. Groaning, he rolled onto his back, keeping their legs together. "It's an ex-lover situation, yes. Although not necessarily regarding the woman herself. Ghosts of the past that are better off left there. Left for dead."

"Yes, but that's your specialty, isn't it? Ghosts?"

His laughter came harsh and dry. "She's the one who got me into paranormal investigation, like I told you. She had a persistence that drew me into my first haunted house that wasn't faked to scare children. The real kind of haunting where you keep your night light on for the next few weeks because you don't want to see what lurks in the shadows. I went to prove her wrong and I stayed to prove her right. Although a part of me has always wanted to see if I could get enough data to blast her life after death theories out of the water."

Instead of feeling spooked, Spring leaned over him, naked as the day she was born, with her breasts pushed against her forearm. The sight drew him immediately. "Tell me more."

"About the woman or the house?"

"Both. Either."

One of them he didn't feel like discussing. Hannah belonged in the past, buried along with the rest of his mistakes, because no relationship Marshall had ever embarked on had worked out in the end. They'd been fifty shades of wrong for him, and he didn't particularly want to bring them up right after coitus.

Especially not with Spring.

Which left...

"You really want to know about my past?" he asked.

She nodded once, eyes wide and curious despite the hour. "It's a give and take deal, Marshall. That's how we learn more about each other."

"And here I'd thought we'd spent the past two hours learning and discovering." He ran a hand along her hip with a blatant invitation in his gaze.

Spring grinned before shifting her position, turning and snuggling until her rear pressed against his pelvis. "We did indeed."

Marshall told her about his first haunted house, about the

initial skepticism and ultimate combination of excitement and angst. The feeling of invisible fingers traveling down his spine and the way he'd been driven to quantify the experience. To put verifiable data to a sensation he hardly knew how to describe.

That experience spurred him into pursuing ghost hunting as a hobby, instead of continuing with his previous derision for what he'd thought of as delusion.

His own interest was engaged and began to refine his investigative technique and get real results when suddenly Hannah dumped him for the charismatic leader of Spirit Hunters, Ax Decker. He had invited Hannah to join the Hunters because his TV show producers insisted that viewers wanted to see a female in the group. God, how Marshall wanted to sock that guy right in the face. It wasn't bad enough that the man took every opportunity to belittle Marshall in public. He also took every opportunity to flaunt how happy he could make Hannah. Something Marshall hadn't been able to do.

He had been devastated when she publicly broke up with him, causing him to have a mini breakdown. A knock-down, drag-out, out of character experience where he couldn't control his actions. Thus the forced "vacation."

"Which reminds me," he said, interrupting himself, "I need to get new equipment today or else the last few days of our experiments will be a bust and I'll head back to New York empty-handed."

Spring's gaze dropped to where she'd looped his hands over her belly. "I really am sorry about what happened at Seafoam House."

Marshall found he hated the way guilt colored her face when he turned to stare at her. Not for the emotions it brought with them on her end, but for how responsible he felt.

"Don't be sorry," he replied, pushing her hair away from

her cheek. "Like I told you, it wasn't your fault. It was probably just some bored kids making trouble because they knew we were trying to do some serious work."

His gut told him a different story, though. Not kids, no, but an issue that had plagued him before.

Could it really be that someone had followed him down from New York? The same someone who had come to his campus for the sole purpose of antagonizing him into a fight?

Marshall shook his head to clear it. He didn't want to think about the Spirit Hunters. Not tonight. Although they'd been on his mind since he'd discovered the break-in.

A sour pit formed in his stomach and it took him a moment longer to realize Spring had asked him a question.

"Do you know where you're going to get the tools you need on such short notice?"

"Some I can order and have them shipped overnight," he told her, catching up in the conversation. "Others I may be able to make myself if I can find the parts."

"Look at you. Professor. Ghost hunter. *Tech genius.*"

"I figure I can use the next few days to get the equipment I need, then run a few more tests before I leave."

Spring shifted, resuming a position next to him. Still able to make eye contact. "Are you sure you don't want to stay longer? I thought you were really starting to like the Bay."

"I do like the Bay," he admitted slowly. "There are so many interesting characters here. And beauty. I guess I didn't expect to like the landscape as much as I do. But I...don't know what I want."

She forced her smile wider. "I'm going to try not to take that personally."

"It's not personal, I promise." Marshall raised up, balancing on his elbow. "If I had a choice, I would spend the entire day in bed with you."

"Doing what?"

"Probably eating pizza and hot wings until I make myself sick."

"I thought you'd had enough of eating challenges," she teased.

He growled and tugged her down so that she lay on her back and he could cover her body with his own. "Maybe it's not actual food I'm hungry for."

"Ooh, you bad boy. Sadly, we both have things to do in the morning." Spring glanced at the clock and sighed. "I have to be at the park in five hours."

"Is your boss going to be mad at you if you're a little late?"

Her grin became wolfish. "I'm sure she will understand." Then she remembered. "Oh, hey."

"Hey yourself."

"There's a huge Halloween bash in a couple of days. They'll have booths set up on the boardwalk, and everyone dresses up in costume. The shops give out candy, there's a costume contest..."

He eyed her skeptically. "I'm not sure I'm up for dressing up in a costume. And why hold it before Halloween?" Hadn't one of the coffee shop ladies told him about it? He vaguely remembered them asking about a costume.

"Because it's a chance to let the kids run around in a safe environment. People really get into it." She wiggled closer in excitement. "I'm going as a black cat."

"It figures." Marshall scoffed, pleased when she bumped his stomach with the back of her hand.

"Come on. It'll be fun!"

"We'll see. There's still a lot we need to do at the house—"

"Things that can wait so that you can experience the full impact of a Cinnamon Bay Halloween extravaganza."

He needed time to mull it over. To see if he wanted to take the chance or not. So he silenced her with a kiss, and let their bodies do the talking.

Spring dragged herself out of her car nearly fifty minutes after she told Mecca she'd be at the park for her shift. Thank God they'd gotten enough extra funds out of their new grants to hire professional counselors. It lifted a lot of weight off Spring's shoulders and left her more flexibility in her hours.

However, as a perpetually punctual Type A personality, Mecca would find it hard to let her friend's tardiness off the hook. Especially not when she found out the real reason for it. Ooh boy, that conversation wasn't going to be fun.

Following the high-pitched sounds of laughter, Spring wound her way around the mess hall toward the cabins and the stretch of beach not far off. The campers were gathered on the sand doing yoga poses on dirtied mats, most of them falling over themselves with laughter and others trying desperately to do a handstand despite the instructor's words of warning.

Her face broke into a smile. Yes, she loved working with the kids. They were a terror half the time and complete lovebugs the rest, and she never got tired of seeing the excitement on their faces, each new group bringing in different personalities.

Pure luck and happenstance had gotten her the position. She'd been traveling through the Bay with her parents in search of a beach rental. A little place they could get away from the bustling city of Charlotte, North Carolina, whenever they needed a break. But Spring had taken one look at the boardwalk and those quaint old ladies inside the coffee shop and decided she didn't just want a beach house getaway. She wanted a life here.

They found and bought the perfect house a few miles away from the boardwalk on a little spit of acreage, and although her parents had later decided it wasn't for them—

they'd rather be free to travel to different places rather than come to the same beach time and again—Spring took the initiative to draw up a rent-to-own agreement.

There was no way she could afford the place by herself outright, and especially not without a job. Things had fallen into place eventually. After a string of odd jobs around the town, she'd landed with Camp Lionheart and never looked back.

That's how she viewed her life, Spring mused, her sneakers crunching over gravel and twigs from the looming pines and oaks. A perpetual line of odd things happening to her while she had no doubt that they would eventually fall into place for her highest good.

She didn't sweat the small stuff.

Which made the tiny tendril of anxiety she felt about Marshall so unnerving. It wasn't related to him as a person. He made her feel safe whenever they were together.

No, her stomach twisted in knots at the thought of him leaving. Of not choosing her. Of ending up as another in a string of bad choices that led to her being alone.

It made no sense, she argued with herself. She'd known it was only temporary when she first met him and had resigned herself to a week or two of fun—if he was agreeable to that, of course—knowing full well he didn't plan to stay.

Spring had never been one to hook her hopes on a man. So what the hell happened?

Marshall happened.

"Hey! You better have a good excuse for being late. Fifty minutes is ridiculous."

The familiar voice of admonishment catapulted Spring out of her thoughts, and when she blinked she saw Mecca striding toward her.

"I was up late last night," she said slowly, adjusting her ponytail and trying not to shrink a few inches under the scrutiny.

"Doing what?"

"Having sex with Marshall."

The statement froze Mecca mid-stride, and the war of emotions on her face was a thing of beauty to behold. "Are you seriously telling me that you got him to sleep with you?"

"*Got him to*, no. He agreed of his own volition. The man's stamina should go down in record books, let me tell you."

Mecca glanced around, saw the kids on the beach, then gestured for Spring to follow. Torn between amusement, curiosity, and a need to be professional, she eventually waved Spring inside the counselors' cabin, hustling the other woman and locking the door behind them. She leaned back to stare at her friend while the tired old ceiling fan clicked overhead with each rotation.

"He had enough stamina to make you late for work?"

"I mean, I don't want to kiss and tell...but sit down!" Spring pointed to the cot in the corner. "I have so much to share!"

She knew better than to get excited over a man. Especially one who'd told her right off the bat that there could be nothing between them. But her own optimism took the reins and led her down that path with merry abandon. She couldn't help but give in to the lurch in her heart, the one that told her she was right about Marshall.

What a surprise, too, because she hadn't thought herself ready for that kind of man. That kind of commitment. She hadn't been sure of *ever* being ready for a package deal and the family that goes along with it. She enjoyed men, yes, but Mr. Right was a thing of myth. He certainly didn't come riding into town on a horse made of refusals and rejections.

Yet here she was, and her gut, which always served to tell her when something had come to its end, was shocked to feel that this was only the beginning.

She ended up telling Mecca everything, her friend watching her with silent and non-judgmental eyes. And though it was good to unload, to have a laugh when needed, it left Spring even more confused than when she'd begun the conversation.

"What are you going to do?" Mecca asked.

Spring bounced on the cot, unable to contain her energy despite her lack of sleep. "About what?"

"About Marshall. *Duh*. Because what other subject have we spent the last—" She glanced at her wristwatch. "—twenty minutes discussing? Ugh, this has really pushed my schedule back."

"I'm going to do nothing," Spring answered simply. "I'm going to just let it flow..."

Mecca's eyes nearly bugged out of her head. "That's the biggest non-answer I've ever heard! What do you mean, let it flow? You mean you're going to let him sleep with you and then waltz away? Come and go as he pleases?"

She'd done it before, hadn't she? "I'm going to do what it is I normally do and see how things progress. Nothing good ever comes from forcing my hand. I mean, do I want to come right out and tell him 'hey, I have the feeling we will be really good partners together, so let's skip right to it and make some babies'? Sure, I've considered saying it."

Spring watched Mecca's eyes get buggier. If that was possible.

"But I'm not going to say anything," Spring continued and jumped to her feet. "I'm going to do my job, help him for as long as I can, and see if the relationship progresses."

Mecca stared at her. "There isn't going to be a relationship if you don't communicate how you feel with him. Right?"

"Let's not press the issue. Isn't it time for us to take the kids on a hike?"

Another glance to the wristwatch. "Damn, you're right. This is what I get for letting you drag me into your gossip."

Spring scoffed. "You enjoyed every minute of it."

"You're right, I did. Now let's wear those little farts out so they can sleep well tonight and give their parents a rest."

Spring trailed behind her friend, wondering if she could be true to her own vow to let things flow. Or if the little tendril of anxiety would grow and grow until she couldn't take the pressure anymore.

CHAPTER TEN

*M*arshall found himself whistling on his way down the boardwalk. One more coffee, he mused, and then he'd be ready to deal with the bullshit of replacing his equipment. He'd already contacted the authorities, who pretty much laughed him off when he told them what he'd been doing at the house. They were the kind of small-minded people who would rather make a joke than take anything outside of their little box seriously.

No matter. He'd come into contact with those types before. Enough times to not let the newest go-round bother him. He had insurance for this type of thing. If he could get his money back for the equipment then it would be worth the struggle.

Although dealing with the insurance company took a bit longer, and the pot of coffee his mother made for him only went so far in easing the tension headache between his eyes. The tension headache caused when she'd interrogated him on his whereabouts the night before.

What could he *possibly* tell her? Nothing good. Nothing that wouldn't have her loudly declaring her disappointment or crying on his shoulder in happiness. She had liked Spring when they'd met at the market. He knew it, as he knew Emmie would berate him for his decision not to proceed with a real relationship.

Just as she disapproved of his paranormal investigations.

Was he doomed to always be seen as a failure in his mother's eyes? At least when it came to his relationships and passions? It was a no-win situation.

Marshall ended up giving his mother a lame excuse before he bolted out of the house, feeling like a teenager. And the clock was ticking down on his time in Cinnamon Bay. He had less than a week left before he had to head back to New York, and he was no closer to cracking the mystery of the Seafoam Street haunting than the first time he'd stepped foot over the threshold.

He still had his handwritten notes, but he'd have to hustle and get that equipment replaced if he wanted to have corroborative scientific data. Not to mention he hadn't interviewed any of the Seafoam Street neighbors yet, hadn't gotten their impressions or, hopefully, eye-witness accounts of the house and the reported paranormal activity associated with it.

So what was he doing wasting time?

His mind drifting inexorably back to his night with Spring, Marshall pushed through the coffee shop door with his lips pursed to whistle a tune only he heard in his head. Or maybe in his heart. If this was wasting time, then maybe he was okay with it. And feeling...happy. Oh yeah.

The Hens turned to him in unison the moment he came through the door. The way they scrutinized him they must have known something was up. Maybe he looked *too* happy.

He approached the counter and the jovial man with dreadlocks hanging down past his shoulders.

"Marshall, right? You've been coming in here often. Jack's nephew." The fellow pointed to the nametag pinned to his black t-shirt. "Kolby."

"Right, nice to officially meet you," Marshall replied with a slight grin.

"Good to see you coming back for more."

Marshall placed his order and waited at the counter. Knowing, *knowing*, the sharks were closing in.

"You can't stay away, can you, boy?"

Yup, there were the gravelly tones he'd come to expect. He turned around to face the first of the women, the one with the pure white curls. "No, I guess I can't. The coffee is too good. It reels me in every time."

Trixie raked him up and down with an all-seeing eye. "You've got something on your mind. Have an interesting night?"

"One could say that." Marshall fought not to blush. How could they possibly tell? Did they have magic powers that could sense when a person got laid? "I had a few setbacks with my investigation at Seafoam House. Nothing more."

Focus on work, he told himself. That way they wouldn't see him sweat.

"A young man like you should *enjoy* your vacation," Birdie admonished. "There's not enough time to work your life away. We told your uncle to take you to the farmers' market. Did you ever make it there?"

"Yes, I went." He nodded in their direction. "Thank you for the suggestion."

"Oh, we are full of suggestions," Hattie stated confidently. "It depends on whether or not you want to take our advice. I have a few things to say about you spending your time at that deplorable house..."

Bestowing the three of them with a warm grin—or else he wouldn't hear the end of it from his uncle—Marshall received his order and paid, counting off bills from his wallet. "It's been fun, ladies, but I've got to go. I hope you have a lovely day."

He hadn't carved out enough of his schedule to waste on

pleasantries—or more accurately, interrogations. If the Hens had their way, he'd join them on one of the stools at the counter and spend the rest of this absolutely beautiful day answering their questions about his personal life.

There were some things a man *had* to keep to himself.

Trixie, Hattie, and Birdie watched him leave, and the latter clucked her tongue. "What are we going to do about that boy?"

Hattie shrugged, the movement causing the whole upper half of her generous body to shift. "Nothing we can do at this point. We've set them in motion. Spring will have to take care of the rest. You know she's good for it."

"She's going to have to move fast," Trixie stated, her eyes following Marshall, still visible through the front window. "There's trouble coming, and this one is more likely to bolt than face it head on. Plus Spring has her own shadows that will certainly come to light before this is over."

"We did our best. They spent the night with each other, didn't they?" Hattie replied irritably.

"One night might not be enough to convince him that he needs her to weather this storm. You've seen him. He's got a noggin tougher than the walls of Fort Knox. He's not convinced she's the right one for him. You can't force someone to see what's right in front of them."

"Have faith, ladies. We've worked our magic." Birdie nodded in one decisive swipe of her pointy chin. "It will be enough."

*M*arshall listened to the march of footsteps behind him, and purposely kept walking without looking over his shoulder. The tingle on the back of his neck told him to get moving. To hurry, to get the equipment he needed before his time ran out. He refused to let anything or anyone throw a wrench in his plans for the day. Least of all himself.

It was hard enough knowing he'd have to look Spring in the eye tonight when she came over to help him. He shook his head, striding across the heated macadam toward his car.

They'd ended up sleeping together. The thought that had filled him with joy moments earlier now sank in a sour pit to the bottom of his stomach.

What had he been thinking?

He'd temporarily lost his mind. That was the only explanation for it. No matter how he'd tried to convince himself it was a terrible idea, he hadn't been able to stop kissing her. Touching her. And then before he knew it...

Bang.

Literally, *bang*.

He stopped, dropping his head against the side of his car and trying to get his brain to focus. Focus on anything other than the smile that haunted his dreams. Had he thought the Seafoam House full of ghosts? His own mind could give the place decent competition.

Hannah...would he ever get her out of his head?

Opening the door with a head full of steam, Marshall spared a moment to sit behind the wheel. He certainly didn't have time to rehash events of the past. Such as the last two investigations he'd gone on with the Spirit Hunters before they decided to cut him out, and how he'd blown his professionalism when Hannah dumped him for Ax Decker then publicly rebuffed him in front of what he'd considered his peers.

His interest had been engaged when he first met her. So lively, bright, full of life. She made him want to be a better teacher, a better man. Or so he'd thought. He was just beginning to refine his investigative technique and get real results from their excursions when suddenly Hannah dumped him for the charismatic leader of Spirit Hunters. Out of the damn blue.

Was he willing to risk his heart again? Risk another Hannah situation? No, he shouldn't have slept with Spring, shouldn't have gone forward with his basest desires. All because he could not get her out of his head.

Marshall pushed his foot down on the gas pedal, his focus on Seafoam House and unloading the back seat full of equipment he'd managed to find. Some pieces he'd have to rig together. Others he'd been able to purchase. More investment in his...hobby.

After opening the lock, he used his foot to shove at the door. Empty silence greeted him, although he expected nothing less. There was something comforting in the feeling. Each new house he chose to investigate gave him the same experience when he first stepped foot over the threshold, that heavy yet reassuring weight that old abandoned houses carried. Marshall didn't feel frightened at the prospect of an honest to goodness haunting. He had never been scared of the dark. The prospect of spirits lingering after death brought a level of excitement he hadn't experienced since teaching his first class, the same kind of thrilling nervousness combined with a tingle beneath his collarbone.

And he knew Spring felt the same way. There was something refreshing about her optimism and wide-eyed enthusiasm. He appreciated those qualities about her, and found himself glancing around the living room even though he knew she wasn't there.

Gah, what was he doing?

Marshall moved into the kitchen, the floor creaking beneath his every step and a strange burning sensation beneath his collarbone. For its age, the house still showed well, and stood strong despite the ravages of the ocean wind. He could feel a slight touch of air on his neck—

He whirled around at the whisper of fingers on his skin.

"Hey!" he called out. More to hear his own voice than anything else, goose bumps bursting to life on his forearm and hair standing on end. "You've got a lot of nerve following me back here. Come on, show yourself."

No answer came.

"Whoever you are, come out." Marshall stomped down the hallway toward the drawing room.

The sensation of eyes on his back stayed with him on his search through the main floor. Hand on the banister, he prepared to climb the steps and scour each room for answers when the front door suddenly slammed shut behind him.

Marshall whirled around, his heart catapulting into his throat.

"Stupid wind," he muttered.

But he spent the rest of the day constantly casting an anxious glance over his shoulder. Waiting for night to fall. Waiting to see if he'd feel those fingertips on his neck a second time.

The electronics, once he got them working, showed no fluctuations in electromagnetic energies. The rest of the tests remained neutral.

He texted Spring to stay home—his only communication with her after their night together.

And when he finally locked up to go home, he wondered at the sensation still plaguing him, rubbing a hand over his neck. The only real ghosts here were the people threatening to make his life a living hell. Seafoam Street, for all the hype surrounding it, appeared perfectly normal.

The type of issue haunting him wasn't something he could easily solve.

CHAPTER ELEVEN

Spring hurried to Seafoam House after her shift ended at Camp Lionheart, only to find the door locked. She peeked in through the front windows and saw nothing on the table they'd set up days earlier. Nothing to indicate that Marshall had come to the place at all.

Curious.

She glanced down at her cell phone to see if he'd left her any more messages beyond the two words telling her not to come. She'd agreed to stay home, texted him back without asking for an explanation. And had yet to receive anything else, the screen coming up blank each time.

Two days later, she tried again, knowing he had to leave to return to New York soon and would be hurrying to gather any last-minute bits of data he might have missed.

Nothing.

The man had ghosted her. Had spit in the face of the help she'd offered.

Other than that simple text, she hadn't heard from him since he'd left her house the night they had made love. Spring tried not to let her good mood slip away at the thought. He was busy, she assured herself. His time in Cinnamon Bay rapidly approached its end, so surely he had a lot of loose strings to tie up.

Why did she get the feeling she had become one of them?

Maybe he intended to meet her at the Halloween party tomorrow night, as they had discussed once. Which was fine, she mused. He'd definitely agreed to check out the Halloween party.

She growled, stopping herself from checking her phone. Again.

The Halloween bash on the boardwalk... It would have to count as a chance to have a conversation. She might not get another, if he wanted to continue acting this way. Like a phantom. Sleeping with her then ditching her. It was not endearing, and there were only so many excuses she could make for him before it became too much.

Anger warred with disappointment and Spring struggled to push both aside as she walked to the car, the house silent and empty in the twilight. She glanced over her shoulder at the sound of knocking. And saw nothing. That one glance assured her that everything was in perfect disordered order.

Nothing out of place.

Which in itself had her spine tingling.

She'd clearly heard four knocks.

"Marshall?" she called out.

Okay, no reason to worry. The slight breeze outside could have sent any number of tree limbs clacking against the side of the house.

She heard a click behind her and when she turned, the door had opened.

Opened on its own? No, impossible. Besides, it was so old and warped it always stuck stubbornly. She craned her neck to see inside, to see if Marshall was playing tricks on her.

"Hello?"

No answer. But that door…

Spring strode forward, making each step deliberately loud. "Marshall, if this is some idea of a stupid joke, I'm not laughing. Why haven't you been answering my texts?"

The wooden porch slats creaked and groaned with her movement. Inside the house, the cool hush was at odds with the heat of the day. The only sound was the faint whine of heat bugs.

"I'm not amused!" Spring yelled into the darkness. Drawn by her curiosity, she stepped inside, making out the dim outline of the staircase.

Not sensing the door closing behind her until it shut.

---

*M*arshall patted his pocket and the cell phone within. He had to stop himself multiple times throughout the day, stop himself from whipping it out and responding to the text messages Spring had sent him.

Yeah, he'd blown her off. After telling her to stay home, he'd hoped she would get the message and keep away from him. It helped him narrow in that focus to the important issues, like the house. Like the family who insisted he wasn't spending enough time with him.

Or so he told himself.

Part of him reeled at the callous behavior. The other part, the one bent on getting quantifiable results at Seafoam House, knew he had to focus and make the best of the few days he had left in Cinnamon Bay. His flight was booked, the shipping already paid for the rest of his equipment to return to New York.

It left him no room for romance. Period. He had nothing to offer, nor did he want to. He had a life in the city and certain expectations for his future. He certainly didn't want to compromise any of that for a chance at heartbreak. Spring and Hannah shared the same kind of kooky enthusiasm. It hadn't worked out the last time, which logically meant he needed to stop beating his head against the proverbial wall and expecting a different outcome.

Perhaps he'd truly gone insane.

Pulling up in front of the house in what had become his designated parking spot, Marshall glanced at the empty windows. The closed front door.

Spring's car was parked across from his own.

He gave himself a neck ache in his haste to look around, the rest of his body still strapped in by the seatbelt. She was here? How did she get *in*?

His camera bag was on the passenger seat, and Marshall grabbed it on his way out, hurrying toward the front door with the keys jingling in his grip.

Fingers shook as he tried to fit the key in the lock. A locksmith had been out here the day after the break-in to change everything. He'd also fixed that broken window. A small measure to try and dissuade the thieves who had come around the first time.

At last the key slid home, and he pushed open the door.

Had Spring broken a window to get in?

"Spring, are you here?" Marshall called out, listening to the echo of his voice through the empty space.

Silence greeted him. The same kind he knew to expect whenever he came here. Only now, with her car outside, he had hoped for a different answer.

A chill crept up his spine and settled at the base of his neck. Maybe she'd parked the car and gone for a walk instead? No, that didn't sound like her.

He dropped the camera bag on the floor and called her name again, a sense of panic tightening in his chest at the lack of answer. He wasn't sure whether he expected one or not at this point. Whether she was playing mind games with him…or not.

A creak from the staircase brought his attention to the living room. "Spring, I'm sorry I didn't answer the phone—" he began.

Then stopped cold when he saw her.

Standing at the foot of the stairs with her hair standing on end in a halo around her. Her arms hung limp at her sides, head thrown back and eyes wide. Unseeing. Her mouth moved on its own, and around her danced shadows. Shadows separate from the darker grays and blacks of the outside palms dancing in the late afternoon sunlight through the windows. Separate from anything he'd ever seen in the past.

His inner investigator urged him to run and grab his camera. To turn his equipment on and get it working because he may never have another opportunity like this. Not when he could clearly see the orbs of light dancing along each riser of the staircase.

As a man, he wanted to give in to the panic and grab her. To shake her out of whatever stupor she'd fallen into. He made to move toward her but came up against an invisible wall. A barrier of his own making, perhaps, but the cold spots his palms pressed against told him otherwise.

"Spring?"

She didn't respond to the sound of his voice. Made no move, with her back arched and hands hanging loose.

Oh no. Dread settled heavily on him. He had to get her out. Now.

Marshall tumbled over himself in an attempt to reach her, his feet tripping over the very air. His heart missed a beat. His eyes, however, missed nothing. They saw every movement of the figure that materialized just one step above the landing, its glassy eyes locked onto Spring.

"Holy fu—"

Marshall gaped as the world slowed around him. Unraveling a piece at a time and trapping him in the present moment. His brain balked at the sight of the specter with one hand outstretched toward Spring.

His own sweaty hand rubbed against the grit in his eyes and, stunned into stupidity, he could only watch.

This was real.

Ghosts...phantoms...were *real*.

His nerves were too keyed up to let him do anything other than watch, to wonder if he could believe his own eyes. It was still too hard for him to wrap his head around this new evidence.

The woman was there yet not there at the same time. A tangible illusion. Marshall saw through her to the wood of the staircase railing, perfectly clear through her torso.

She stood phantom-white, long hair washed out and pupils missing. Marshall made out the vague outline of a dress, the material slowly shifting around her as though suspended in water.

His lips parted and although he wanted to call out, to drag Spring away from the ghost creeping ever closer, he could only manage her name.

Morbid fear broke through the shock and he lunged forward, forcing a shaky breath into his lungs. The next step he took had the barrier bursting, dust raining down and the ghost woman vanishing in a ripple of movement.

He jolted forward just in time to catch Spring as she collapsed. She'd lost her color, the normal rosy glow to her cheeks gone. Noise returned to Seafoam House and it was only then that Marshall realized how still everything had gone in those moments before. No insects chirping. No birds calling out to their mates. If it hadn't been for the ragged beat of his heart echoing in his ears, Marshall might have thought he'd lost his hearing.

"Spring, talk to me." He tapped against her cheek. "Say something, damn it. Please."

He ignored the soft *tap*, *tap* coming from the top of the stairs. He didn't want to see what stood there, what kind of creature lurked, with their knocking demand.

His eyes burned as he watched Spring. To see if her chest rose, if her pulse steadied.

The rational part of his brain was already coming up with an excuse for what he'd seen, despite his years of hoping for exactly this scenario. His eyes must have been playing tricks on him. The apparition of a woman had been nothing but an illusion, the tapping from the stairs a wayward branch on the outside of the house.

Had he been drinking at all? Nope, not a drop, not even the daily minimum requirement of water.

His mind spiraled in circles, searching for answers that he didn't have. He hadn't even bothered to turn on the equipment. Any evidence he might have gathered during the incident was lost unless he could find a way to duplicate it again.

But after he'd seen the way Spring had frozen, the way her skin felt like ice, even the rational part of his mind had abandoned that idea.

His heart nearly burst out of his chest when Spring took a shaky inhale. Then opened her eyes.

Marshall counted the heartbeats until her gaze met his, swallowing over the massive lump in his throat. He raised a hand to her forehead and smoothed away the wayward strands of hair.

"You had me worried," he began shakily.

Empty eyes stared into his, as though she couldn't quite remember him, couldn't return fully to the present moment. He bit the inside of his cheek and waited. Willed himself not to be sick with worry over her.

Bad enough he was clammy and trembling. Some ghost

hunter he'd turned out to be. And a worse protector, if Spring were any indication.

Her lips trembled, teeth clenching as tears sprang from the corners of her eyes.

"She died here, Marshall." The statement, whispered, packed a nearly physical punch. "She died here, and they just left her."

CHAPTER TWELVE

*S*pring couldn't feel her toes. Couldn't feel much of anything, for that matter. The moment she'd stepped over the threshold into the house, her entire body had gone numb, and it wasn't until she'd woken up to Marshall's insistent tapping on her face that she realized where she was. What had happened. And the terrible knowledge of the past had filled her with an unshakable sadness.

Marshall helped her into a seated position, and it was only once she assured him she could handle herself that he left long enough to grab a thermos of coffee and pour her a cup. She'd knocked it over, her fingers trembling and unable to hold the cup, the liquid spilling across the wooden floor and forcing Marshall to scurry to refill the cup for her.

Ghosts are real, aren't they?

Ghosts *were* real, and she'd seen one. Not only seen one. Had felt the woman's fear. Her sorrow and her desolation.

Spring searched her soul for any negative residual emotions attached to the experience, but beyond a little worry about her own reaction, she felt nothing. The woman's spirit hadn't seemed evil or malevolent in any way. She hadn't tried to worm her way inside Spring's body and take over.

In fact, it was the ghost's own emotions that stuck out the most.

Spring accepted the second cup Marshall handed her with a tremulous smile.

"Are you...going to tell me what happened?" he asked slowly. Eyes averted and landing on the same spot on the staircase where the woman had been.

He'd had the wherewithal to turn on the equipment, and they were both on high alert for any signs of the ghost. Call it intuition. Call it a wild guess. But Spring knew they wouldn't see any more of the woman tonight.

Is she trapped here?

She tilted her head up and stared at him. "I'm not exactly sure myself." Her voice sounded rusty. Unused. Clearing her throat, she tried again. "I came by to talk to you and the door was locked. I was about to leave and it just...opened."

Marshall scowled down at her. "Impossible."

The quirked eyebrow she sent him argued the point without words. At last he sighed, running his hands through his hair. "I guess it's not impossible," he admitted. "I wouldn't have thought so if I hadn't seen...her."

"I don't know her name. I just know how she felt in the final moment. How she died here." It felt surreal to sit there, calmly sipping coffee while her entire worldview was shaken to its very foundation. The rush of caffeine helped quiet her mind. Bring her back to herself.

"You said she died here. I don't have any research notes about a woman who passed away in the house."

Marshall's rational argument grew out of his own insecurity, she knew. He wanted to get to the bottom of this. To figure out what had happened and slap a label on it. A label Spring knew couldn't possibly encompass the whole of the experience.

"You aren't going to find her in your notes. She fell down

the stairs and cracked her skull. Her husband and daughter didn't find her until it was too late."

"Husband and daughter..." Marshall trailed off, then scrambled for his notes. He pushed blond hair out of his face, flipping through the typed pages he'd printed off, searching. Searching for what, Spring didn't know.

"I'm not sure how I know, but I'm right," Spring insisted.

His index finger tapped a page. "You told me people have mentioned the apparitions of a tall older gentleman and a young girl."

"Yes, but the sense I got...*they* didn't die in the house. She's the only one who's trapped here. And she's still looking for them."

Spring could almost see the wheels spinning in his brain. "So if they didn't die here, then...what if those aren't ghosts at all, but rather *her* apparitions of a sort? What if a young wife and mother died tragically in the house at some point in the past, and it is *her* spirit that is unable to rest because she constantly searches for her husband and daughter, possibly feeding her energy to the residual memories?"

"It would explain the cold spots. The shadows, the electromagnetic activity in that area."

"I have here that Thomas Strauss built the house, then moved his wife and young daughter in. He and his daughter Matilda moved out suddenly a few years after it was built. And since then, well, you know the stories. No one has been able to live here for any length of time without reporting strange sightings. But no mention of what happened to the wife and mother."

Spring stared down at her hands. They'd finally gone still, the warmth of the coffee seeping through her skin to unthaw her bones. "They must have moved out of the house right after her death because it was too painful to remain. But why no mention of a wife in any of the property deeds? Surely it would have mentioned that there were three of them living here instead of just a father and daughter."

"I couldn't answer that," Marshall said.

The pieces clicked into place in a way they hadn't been able to until now. "So the sightings of the man and girl are only residual energy aided by the ghost mother still searching for them. It makes sense, doesn't it?" Speaking it out loud helped. It helped her remain calm when she would have started freaking out about her connection to the place. How the ghost had somehow chosen her to communicate with. And what it meant for her future.

Marshall crouched down in front of her, balancing on the tips of his toes, sneakers white against the dulled and graying floor. "You're a natural catalyst, Spring. I'm not sure why things only happen when you're around, but they do. And I think together we can tackle this and find a resolution."

She stared at him, wanting to be angry for the way he'd blown her off before. Wanting to strike out at him verbally and remind him that the game he played with her emotions wasn't fair. She did none of those things. Only swallowed, smiled, and nodded. "We can help her move on."

"If that's what you want."

More than anything. Slowly, she nodded, and Marshall held out a hand to help her to her feet. They worked as a team, setting up the equipment in anticipation of replicating the phenomenon from before.

Even when the house remained silent.

The next night, Spring applied makeup and drew liner around her eyes to cat-like perfection. Graceful black ears on a headband blended in with hair she'd straightened into a sleek ponytail down her back. Around her waist, she'd looped a sash of black felt that fell down to the back of her knees like a tail. Hugging her curves, the black leotard showed off her figure, snug in all the right places.

An attempt to get back to her normal self after a soul-shaking paranormal encounter.

Spring blew herself a kiss in the mirror. *Let Marshall weep*, she thought with a devilish grin. She'd certainly show him what he'd miss if he were to return to New York permanently. And make him understand that he'd made a mistake in disappearing on her. No need for hysterics. No need to get emotional and make a scene.

Let her actions—and his—speak for themselves.

Then she sighed, as if her sails deflated. How foolish could a person be, thinking that someone else would give up his entire life based on one night of sex. *Great* sex, yes, but he had a job he loved in New York. An apartment, friends. A routine. A life.

Her mind ran in circles the entire drive to the boardwalk, where she realized she should have walked instead of gotten lazy. There were no parking spaces, everything taken up by vehicles packed with frenzied party-goers.

How could she have forgotten? The entire town showed up for the boardwalk bash. It was tradition.

In the span of a day, Cinnamon Bay had transformed from coastal playground into a Halloween wonderland. Orange lights and plastic pumpkins were strung through the palm trees along the boulevard closest to the boardwalk, cones and partitions blocking or detouring traffic. The sun had yet to fully set, casting deep peach and violet rays over the crowds already flocking the sidewalks.

Children and adults alike dressed as monsters and vampires. Ghosts and superheroes.

Spring spent another fifteen minutes trying to find a place to park before giving up and driving home, determined to walk this time. Her knees and ankles protested vehemently.

Yet it was worth it for those first strands of laughter once she got close enough to hear them. It brought a smile to her face.

The noise, the heat, the fun...she needed it. Needed it to stop thinking about Marshall, and the ghost in Seafoam House. The ghost desperate to find her family and trapped with no release.

She knew the feeling.

She swished her tail as she cut through the crowd, heading toward the coffee shop. There were children bobbing for apples along the boardwalk, dressed in their costumes and laughing their heads off, with parents clustered nearby. The stores had gone crazy with decorations. There were plastic witches cackling and pumpkins and gourds carved, black and orange lights everywhere.

Several people reached out for conversation, and she engaged. All the while searching the crowd for Marshall. Her fingers itched to text him until she remembered the fact that the leotard had no pockets. She'd left everything except for a wad of cash at home.

She hurried forward. Wishing—*hoping*—Marshall waited for her.

<hr>

*M*arshall had to act fast. He'd spent the last day locked inside of Seafoam House, trying desperately to learn her secrets and coming up with nothing. Not like he had when Spring was with him.

He hadn't gotten anything close to those readings since, and not for lack of trying. Nor had the ghost woman materialized for him again.

His new equipment worked like a charm. Or so he thought until he kept getting the same neutral readings. Checking repeatedly that they were functioning properly brought him no closer to the results he desired. Neither did burrowing his nose in regional history books about the shipwreck which provided the wood used to build the house.

He spent countless hours reading about the people who had lived and died in the house, countless more hours researching the Strauss family. Only on one obscure website did he find a mention of Thomas's wife, the woman Spring claimed had died in the house.

Anastasia Strauss.

The entry made no mention of her death, only saying the woman had been plagued with mysterious illnesses that kept her mostly confined to bed after the birth of her first and only child, Matilda.

Small details began to make sense to him. Why the entries he'd read on Thomas Strauss said the man rarely let visitors into the home. How he did not even employ a maid or servants to tend to his family despite their wealth. They were the actions of a man desperately clinging to his memory of a healthy wife, a man afraid of the embarrassment, the judgment of his community.

Marshall leaned back in his chair, wiping at his eyes. A glance at the clock told him it was approaching nine pm. Time to get his rear over to the house to see what he could do. It was his last full night in town. He grabbed at the phone—

Spring.

He'd meant to call her earlier and had completely forgotten in his quest for knowledge. She'd be utterly pissed at him, as though she weren't already. They still hadn't made any mention of their sleeping together the other night. Or the fact that he meant to leave tomorrow.

Then he remembered. The boardwalk holiday boo bash.

Fuck, he'd completely spaced. Spring had told him to meet her there before they began their experiments for the last time. Told him to meet her at the coffee shop...at seven.

Oh boy. Two hours late.

"Why didn't you tell me it was so late?" he griped at Emmie on his way out the door.

She held a plastic pumpkin in her hands, still half full of candy. "It's *my* job to make sure you're on time now? You're an adult, Marsh. Start acting like one."

Yeah, he should. The problem was he couldn't seem to get himself in hand.

This was probably a bad idea to go, he reminded himself, adjusting the set of his jacket as he walked toward Brew with a View. Going to this costume party at her behest was definitely a bad idea. She'd surely be mad again when she saw him, after his disappearing act. After the way he'd blown hot and cold since the moment they met.

He'd taken great pains to distance himself from her. She would hate it, he knew. *Did* hate it. But he remained adamant. He was in no place to get into another relationship, especially not with someone who reminded him so much of Hannah.

Once he left town, Spring could go back to her old life, as would he.

And yet she was connected to the house, and with her there, Marshall had experienced something completely unprecedented.

Despite the late hour, there was still a large crowd on the boardwalk. He glanced around with a scowl, but the expression slowly melted off his face at the pure joy he witnessed. The joy countless people had always told him was missing from his own life.

He worked his way toward the coffee shop. This was *such* a bad idea. And a waste of time. He would leave for home tomorrow afternoon, and with his notes still woefully incomplete on the haunting, he should have been focusing his energies on that instead of finding an acceptable costume. Especially when he'd ended up in an old dress tux of his uncle's with a lame backstory to boot.

Evil villain? It fit him, Marshall supposed.

A tug on his arm had him whirling around, ready to kiss or kill depending on who the hand belonged to.

He decided on neither when he looked down at Birdie.

"And who are you supposed to be tonight?" the old woman croaked reproachfully. Her dark eyes were shadowed with kohl and he vaguely recognized the jingling chains around her wrists, ankles, and waist. A belly dancer?

"I'm an evil mastermind," Marshall answered kindly, struggling to make himself overheard above the spooky soundtrack blasting through the speakers. "Doesn't it fit?"

Birdie stared at him from top to bottom—and a few in-between places that had him squirming under the scrutiny. "I suppose it will have to do."

"Where are the rest of your cronies?"

Birdie shrugged and the beads of her dress shifted, changing colors under the holiday lights strung above them. "They're around. Making sure the peace is kept around here."

"Then you must be working overtime."

"She's inside, you know." Birdie sniffed. "She's been waiting for you."

Marshall stiffened. "I'm not sure who you're talking about."

Birdie pinched his arm. "Then you don't deserve the title of mastermind, *genius*. Get inside and tell that girl how you feel."

He resented the fact that the woman felt she had a right to tell him what to do. Just as he resented the push she gave him that, strangely enough, propelled him forward. Her arms didn't look strong enough for any kind of muscle.

Besides, there was nothing to say, he thought grimly as he walked inside the coffee shop amidst the frenzied energy of candy-seeking children in their costumes. He enjoyed Spring's company, yes. He liked her work ethic and the way her smile brought warmth and light to his heart. But they both knew a future together was impossible.

Still, he searched for her. Feeling like a fool in a borrowed tux, more so after his behavior of the last few days. Why had he come? He should have sent her a text asking her to meet him at the house and forgone this bullshit boo bash altogether.

Marshall spared a glance over his shoulder. He could still make a run for it. Take off before anyone else saw him and pretend he'd come down with a cold or something. Maybe he could even get a few more hours of research in before—

"Where have you been? Do you have any idea how late you are?"

Her voice came out of nowhere and Marshall nearly jumped out of his skin. When he finally turned to her, he had one hand on his chest to try and still his runaway heart. "Christ, woman, are you trying to kill me? Why did you sneak up on me like that?"

Spring grinned, twining her costume tail around her fingers and drawing his attention to the black leotard clinging to her body and very effectively showing off her considerable assets.

His mouth went dry. His heart stuttered before resuming pounding to beat the band.

"Because it's more fun that way," she replied easily. The fake whiskers on her cheeks twitched when her grin grew wider. "Actually, I called your name but you must have been lost in your head and didn't hear me. Thinking some deep thoughts?"

"You could say that," Marshall muttered. Then he steeled himself for the nagging, emotional lecture he expected. A lecture like Hannah had loved giving him when he lost himself in work and forgot to call her for days at a time and she didn't feel herself a priority in his life.

Not that it made her wrong.

But his stomach dipped to his feet anyway.

Spring dropped her tail and linked her arm through his

with a small smile. "I'm glad you came tonight. I didn't think you would make it. Rather, I thought you'd make it a point to stay home and blow me off the way you have been doing lately."

"I'm sorry."

"Did you still want to get one more night of work in?" she asked.

"Yeah, about that..." He trailed off, running a hand through his hair. "I wanted to talk to you—"

She stopped, face dropping. Immediately on guard, Marshall reached out for her against his better judgment.

"What's wrong?"

"I...don't know." Her hand went to her stomach. "I suddenly feel weird."

"You've been overindulging in candy, haven't you?"

His joke went unheeded. "The house." Dark eyes rose to meet his. "We need to get over there now."

"Yeah, we're going. I meant to be here earlier and I completely forgot, but we still have time for some last-minute tests, as long as you don't mind staying up til the wee hours of dawn."

"No, Marshall. We need to leave. *Right*. *Now*. Someone is trying to break in."

CHAPTER THIRTEEN

He didn't ask her how she knew. Didn't question her connection to the house, not when he'd seen it for himself. If Spring told him they needed to go, then he would follow her without hesitation.

"Okay then." Grabbing her hand, he fought to blaze a path through the crowd. "I've parked pretty far away," he told her over his shoulder.

"I walked. We're not going to make it in time."

He refused to let anyone break into that house again. Not when they might stand a chance of stopping them. His insides torn between fury and fear, he lifted an arm out in front of him to physically push people aside.

"You two look like you're in a hurry! Leaving so soon?" Birdie stepped in front of Marshall and blocked his path. A wrinkled battering ram ready to pummel him if he didn't give her the right answer.

Marshall opened his mouth to make an excuse when Spring cut in front of him. "We need to get to Seafoam House. Do you still have your handicap plates?"

It took him a moment to follow and understand what she

meant by the question. Still felt ridiculous as he watched Birdie nod.

"If you need an escort with a great parking spot, then I'm your gal. Come on."

The three Hens fell in line together. With Hattie's heft leading the way, the crowd parted and allowed them to pass. Spring tried to hurry, and Marshall had to slow her steps to keep up with the three older ladies.

Birdie's van was parked just below the entrance to Bay Freeze. Prime real estate in a lot jammed with cars and trucks.

"Let me just see where I put my keys." She patted down her flattened front.

"Here, you old fool." Hattie reached down into her own ample bosom and withdrew a set of keys. "We drove together tonight."

"I'm taking the front seat," Trixie insisted.

Without time to waste, Spring and Marshall scrambled into the musty confines of the van, watching the door creak closed behind them. Birdie reversed out of the parking lot and nearly hit a Smart Car in her way, then bolted out into the street.

"Easy does it," Hattie admonished when Birdie bumped the curb.

Marshall leaned close to whisper in Spring's ear. "She drives like my uncle."

But Spring paid him no attention, her gaze focused on the road in front of them and her knuckles clenched white.

Birdie got them to the house in record time, just as a brick came flying through one of the front windows.

"Those little bastards are going to pay," Marshall growled through his teeth.

The second Birdie stopped the van, he was out the door, Spring hot on his heels with her black cat tail swaying behind her.

"I'm going to punch someone in the throat!" she threatened.

"Let's not be too hasty!" he tried to warn her. But as usual, Spring didn't listen. She charged ahead and stood in front of the very closed, very locked front door.

What if she was wrong about a break-in? No, the goose bumps on her arms and hair standing straight up at the nape of her neck told her she'd been right. Not to mention the brick they'd seen sailing through one of the front windows as they'd pulled up.

"*Hurry*," she urged.

He fumbled in the pockets of his borrowed suit for where he'd stashed the keys, dropping them like a wide receiver bungling the last pass in a tied football game with two seconds left on the clock. He finally got the key in the lock and twisted, the door whooshing open with a breath of air. A sigh. The wind moaning around them.

"Marshall…"

He kept her behind him when she obviously wanted to charge ahead without thinking. "Whoever you are, you're going to have to come out now! You're trespassing. And if you break my things again, I swear to God there will be swift and brutal retribution."

The punch came at him from the right, muscles tensed and a hand bunched into a fist slamming into his nose.

Marshall staggered and went down on his knees, blood dripping through the fingers he pressed to his nose.

He hadn't expected the ambush. Liked the pain even less. He saw little through the red haze of anger as he rose to his feet.

"Come on. You want to be a big man, come here and break into my site? Destroy my equipment? Well, come at me and let's see what you've got!"

The man wore a ski mask to cover his features, a duffel

bag slung over his left shoulder. A glance at the table where the equipment used to sit revealed its surface cleared.

The thief certainly didn't expect Marshall to rise and launch himself forward, catching the man around the midsection and sending them both toward the staircase. Wood cracked when they collided against the banister but held beneath their combined weight, halting their progress and sending a wave of agony through him.

An elbow dug into his neck and he cried out. *Damn it, that hurts!*

"Marshall, stop. Please."

He glanced over to see Spring's face. Not angry at him, as he expected. No. She was terrified. Staring behind them with her eyes focused on someone, or something, else.

The temperature around them dropped. A chill sent shudders through him as he turned to face the man in the ski mask. Dark eyes stared back at him, a white flash where the man's teeth were bared.

Prickles rose on the back of his neck and Marshall squinted into the darkness. Past the assailant, to where moonlight poured in through the front windows to highlight a faint outline of a figure. A woman.

He flicked his gaze from the ghost to Spring. She stood behind him, twisting her fingers together.

Trapped, Spring had said. The woman was trapped here waiting for her family to come back. What would she think of the man who'd broken in?

"You're going to want to leave this house before something dreadful happens to you," Marshall told the man calmly.

He received a sneer in return. "Why? You got the cops called?" The gravelly tenor was unfamiliar.

"No. But someone doesn't take kindly to your presence here."

"Marshall..." Spring began.

"What the hell are you talking about?" The man hefted

the bag over his shoulder and used his other hand to reach behind him for a knife. The blade glinted in the moonlight. "You think you and the woman can take me?"

Fear squeezed his insides. But he couldn't afford to give in to it. A single bit of weakness could mean serious injury for both of them. For Spring. And that was an unforgivable cost.

"You might want to look behind you." Marshall ignored the ache in his face, thinking through his next move. He should have called the cops right away. On the drive over. Maybe he could use the element of surprise.

The sensors in the duffel bag began to beep, although none of them, surely, had been turned on. The thief jolted with surprise, and as he twisted to shift the bag, he caught sight of the apparition.

Marshall noted the moment comprehension filled the thief's face. The ghost behind them didn't move. Didn't need to. She stood staring down with blank features, her white dress drifting as if on an invisible current, flowing hair a luminous white distinctly apart from the shadows. And in the darkness glowed two angry eyes.

Marshall swallowed hard, knowing he'd never get used to seeing her. Hoping he would never have to. He took a step back and tried to imagine what the man thought. From the sounds of labored breathing, the way he began to shake, it wasn't anything good.

"What the fuck—"

Any desire to finish the sentence passed in a blink. The man dropped the duffel bag and bolted past Marshall and Spring out the front door, an unnatural chill following him, one that cut to the bone. Mist spilled down the staircase and trailed around their feet.

Wiping the side of his face with his sleeve, Marshall stared at the blood and winced. His breath was a cloud of vapor.

"Can you tell her to stop?" he asked Spring, not entirely sure if he'd lost his mind or not.

She stared at him and slowly nodded. "I'll try." Her voice came out a whisper, and she closed her eyes. Released the fists she'd made and let her hands hang loose.

The cold lessened, a feather-light touch slipped across the back of his neck, and when Marshall looked again at the top of the stairs, the space was empty. He blinked as though it might conjure the outline of the figure once more.

With a sigh he turned back to Spring. "You should have stayed in the car. It wasn't safe in here."

She gave her head a small, quick shake that had him frowning. "I wasn't going to let you fight alone. Knowing you, you'd rather bash the man's teeth in than do this the right way."

Marshall sighed again, raised a hand to his hair and noticed the sweat on his forehead. The motion made him flinch. Damn, the guy had done a number on his nose. Pretty ballsy move for someone who broke into the same house not once but twice. "If your *friend* hadn't scared me, I would have."

"I wouldn't necessarily call her a friend, Professor. Gosh." Spring raised a hand to her chest. "My heart is beating a mile a minute. I can't seem to breathe."

That's when Marshall realized he'd let this go on for too long.

"Sit down," he told Spring firmly. "Before you fall down."

She opened her mouth to argue, then folded her arms over her chest. "I'm not sitting down here. The Hens are still outside. I think we should head back out and make that call."

The police. Yeah, he'd need to alert them, see what they found at the scene. And hope he hadn't made things worse with the scuffle.

A throat cleared and brought their attention to the doorway.

"We're going to leave you kids here to settle this mess," Birdie stated, peering inside. As though she was unwilling to go inside the house. In fact, the three of them had stopped in the doorway and would come no farther.

Spring inclined her head. "Thank you again for giving us a ride over here. It's appreciated."

"One last thing before we get back to the coffee shop and out of this mess for good," Hattie asserted. She shifted to face Marshall, her expression stern and ready to brook no argument. "Ask your uncle to give you some pointers on fighting, if that's what you intend to do in your spare time."

Birdie nodded in agreement. "That way you won't go down like a sack of potatoes."

Marshall tried to smile and found that the action hurt. When he dipped his tongue out to check, it came away tasting of copper. His lip must have split. "Thank you for the advice. I'm sorry you had to see that."

"Make sure it doesn't happen again," Trixie warned. "You need to take better care of your things, boy. And invest in a good set of locks if you're going to leave them lying around for any would-be thief."

The three of them moved as a unit back toward the van.

He stared at the bag the thief had dropped, still filled with his equipment. The same equipment that had now gone silent.

"Come on, Professor." Spring, who had been oddly quiet until then, shifted to steer them both outside and toward the curb so they could sit down. "Let's see if we can clean you up while we wait for the cops."

The first step had him wincing in pain. "That bastard got me right in the 'nads with his knee."

"I'm not surprised. You were tussling like toddlers before the ghost showed up. I'd be willing to bet you have splinters in your ass, too."

"There might be a few," he conceded with an attempt at a grin.

The humor left him. He couldn't subject her to this. Not when he knew he was leaving.

Right or not, they'd been a team tonight. Her ties to the house, her ties to him...Marshall wasn't sure what to do about either one. It hurt worse, though, finally acknowledging how much he cared for her.

He'd bungled everything.

"Easy does it." She helped him down the steps, the black tail swinging behind her.

"You don't have to help me," he said at last. "I'm fine. He didn't hit me that hard."

"What am I going to do? Leave you here? We saw the same things. My statement will be just as important to the police. Besides, with you mending this broken nose, I'll snoop around the outside for clues."

Snoop for clues while he sat there like a lump? He wouldn't have known about the break-in without her. And he hadn't been able to do anything when the thief threw the first punch.

It took great effort to extract himself from her arms. "I can walk on my own, thanks."

Spring stared at him for a moment before dropping her chin in a short nod. "I know what it's like to feel helpless, Marshall." The words came out soft. "Trust me."

"What?"

"Feeling helpless," she repeated bitterly. "I know how it feels when you think control has been taken away. When you feel like the situation has gone beyond what you should be able to handle."

His heart sank. Her latest revelation made this so much harder than it already was. "Spring..."

Her gaze lifted to his, though her eyes gave nothing away. "Yes?"

"I'm leaving town," he forced himself to say.

"I know." Of course she did.

"I don't know when—even *if*—I'll be back."

Her head dipped toward the ground, the right cat ear flopping with the motion. "Again, something I already know."

"I'm not planning on getting into a relationship anytime soon. Whatever this is," he gestured between them, "was fun while it lasted. But it's time to put it to an end. I'm sorry I disappeared on you. I'd hoped to make this easier by staying away."

"Really?" She surprised him by laughing, the sound cool and dry. "If you think you're protecting me by pushing me away, then think again. I'm not going anywhere. We'll handle this together."

He stopped her when she tried to step close. "I'm not trying to protect you. I'm serious. That's why I haven't returned any of your calls or texts. That's why I ghosted you. Because us sleeping together made me realize how impossible this is. We're too different. We are different people with different ways of thinking and being and doing."

"Is that really how you feel?" she asked slowly, plainly.

No condemnation. No pleading. Just a simple question. Oh, this was so much worse. He'd rather take her fury, her rage. Her arguments on why they made sense together. His heart lurched with a painful thud.

"Yes," Marshall forced himself to say. "That is really how I feel. I'm sorry, Spring. I appreciate your help with the house, I do. But you're not the girl for me. If it was right, then I would have felt it by now." He shook his head. "I'm truly sorry."

"Make no mistake, Marshall. Once I'm out…I'm *gone*," she replied. Her arms hung limp at her sides. "I'm not coming back."

He swallowed hard. "Who says I want you to come back?"

"Oh, you can try to fool yourself with that garbage, but I

know better. You are going to be sorry from the moment I walk away. And you will, I guarantee it, spend the rest of your days wondering how your life might have been if you'd taken a chance with me."

"Spring—"

She pointed over her shoulder. "I'm going to leave now, because there are too many things going on in my head to be around you for much longer. This is your last chance to try and stop me."

He gave in to his own anger, because it was better than the fear. The fear and the guilt and the utter sadness at losing her. Losing her by his own choice. "I never wanted this in the first place!" he exclaimed. "I never wanted any of this, the romance or the ties or the desire. None of it! And here you are telling me that *you're* leaving, when *I'm* the one packing up to go. Does any of this make sense to you?" Marshall gripped his temples, his hands close to ripping the hair from his head.

"Are you done?" she asked stiffly.

"I...I don't know what I'm doing anymore. I don't know whether I'm coming or going, and you expect me to make a life-changing decision on the spur of the moment, like it's that simple."

"It *is* that simple. You either know," Spring paused to shrug, "or you don't. I'm not going to waste my time on someone who isn't sure about me. If you want to leave, then by all means leave. Go back to the Hannahs of the world. They aren't going to make you happy."

"You knew how I felt when we started this and I'm telling you again that this isn't going to work."

She stared at him for a moment longer, saying nothing. Keeping still. A living statue made of an emotion he could not name. Different from the woman who had run to him that first day. Worlds apart from the one he'd taken to bed days ago. "Like I said. *Simple*. Goodbye, Marshall."

He didn't stop her when she turned away from him. As he

didn't stop her when she walked down the street, her own house many blocks away. Quietly. A whisper in the night.

Like that, she was gone. Out of his life. For good, she'd said.

He scoffed because it was better than the humiliation of running after her. It was certainly better than getting down on his knees and begging her to forgive him for being an ass. Neither one held any appeal, and his pride kept him rooted in place as though he'd dunked his sneakers in cement and let it dry.

And yet...that was it? No big fight, like he'd expected when Hannah left him for Ax? No big scene where she pleaded with him, begged him to reconsider?

No. Spring did not plead. Or beg.

Once she made up her mind, it was done.

He was done.

His choice, right?

It had to be this way, Marshall reasoned, slipping his hands into his pockets and slowly stalking back to the front door he'd left wide open, fumbling for his phone. He'd known from the start there could never be anything between them.

A whirlwind blew leaves past him on a stiff breeze and he kicked the threshold, his tolerance for any of this shriveled and dead.

CHAPTER FOURTEEN

*S*pring barely looked up at the squeal of tires four days later. People tended to drive into the parking lot near the campgrounds like they were preparing to race in the Indy 500. It nearly gave her heart palpitations at the thought of the campers playing anywhere near the asphalt when those maniacs came through, but today she didn't look up for more than a second.

"Geez, watch where you're going!" she called out as the Honda Accord screeched into a parking spot near the end of the lot.

People needed to learn that they couldn't act the fool whenever they wanted, Spring thought, shaking her head as she turned toward the mess hall. But that brought her mind automatically back to Marshall and his nasty performance.

It had played on repeat the entire night of the Halloween bash, taking her under like a riptide of emotion and keeping her stuck there. Swirling. Drowning. The next morning, when bright sunlight shone down and stung her swollen eyes, she'd forced those feelings aside. If she couldn't find things in her life to be happy about, then she didn't deserve the blessings she had.

Marshall Rownan could take a flying leap. If he preferred to push her away, thinking it the best move, then *her* next move was to be even happier than before.

No question about it.

"Nope, he's out of my mind!" She swiped her hands through the air, then swung her arms around in a large circle. "Totally out of my mind. For good."

She hadn't gone back to the Seafoam Street house, either, although the draw had been there. The tug at her mind reminding her of the very real, very strange connection she felt to the house and the woman trapped inside of it. But Spring couldn't bear the thought of standing on that front porch without Marshall by her side.

Eventually he would find his way back to the house, and perhaps she would even join him. A haunting like that meant he wouldn't stay away for long. Not when there was still so much work left to do, tests left to run, experiences left to document. And that poor lost spirit who still needed help.

Their help.

Her heart dropped low. Could she stomach working with him again, knowing he didn't really want to be with her?

It might be more than she could stand, and no matter what happened in her life, Spring knew she could tolerate a whole lot of bullshit. Except when it came to him.

A throat cleared behind her.

"Spring."

Her name. One syllable, and her lower extremities melted. She didn't need to turn around to see who stood behind her. Who had more than likely been the one driving the car that raced into the parking lot moments before.

She stifled a groan and turned slowly around.

Marshall was here. Standing with his hands at his sides, blond hair ruffled and blue button-up shirt left open at the top. He'd come back.

Not for her, because that kind of bullshit only happened

in the movies. She'd lived long enough to know that real life wasn't the movies, and men didn't suddenly step up. They were emotionally incapable.

So what in fresh hell was he doing here? And why did he have to look so good?

"Get out of here," Spring demanded. "You aren't welcome."

"Am I not?" Marshall asked, stepping closer.

Spring boxed his ears. Not violently, just emphatically.

"Go away! I'm done with these games. These stupid testosterone games. You think you can act however you want without a care for who gets caught in the crossfire?" She gestured between them. "Figure it out on your own. I'm done."

She couldn't stop the tears as she turned and strode away, her stomach flipping over itself.

Footsteps trailed after her, running to catch her. "Spring, wait."

"Not a chance," she yelled and kept her gaze on the ground directly ahead of her and her feet moving steadily toward the mess hall. Heaven forbid he see her crying. That was the last thing she wanted or needed.

"Please. I need to talk to you."

"There's nothing left to talk about," she insisted. "I think we've pretty much hashed out everything between us."

"Please!"

She stopped, her fists curling into balls at her sides. Marshall stood close. Too close for her liking. She could smell the cologne he'd spritzed probably as an afterthought, but it was enough to have her stupid heart tripping over itself yet again. "I thought you were leaving town," she said at last.

"Yeah, I thought I was too. I made it all the way to the airport before I changed my mind."

She still couldn't look at him. "Well, why don't I throw you a parade?"

Nope, too bitter. She had to keep control over her emotions, not let him rattle her.

"I know you're a little upset with me right now—"

Big mistake. "A *little*?" Her forehead wrinkled and the rest of her alternately stilled and jumped into action, whirling around to face him. "Marshall, I want to strangle you! Get your head out of your ass if you can't see what a catch I am." She released a groan. "Never mind. I am an amazing person and I don't need to beg a man for his attention. If you don't want to be with me, then that's your issue, not mine. There's something wrong with your mind if you think you can find anyone better than me. *I* can do better, sure, but *you* can't."

"Spring—"

"I'm not done with my tirade," she continued, jumping back when he moved toward her. Needing to keep distance between them while this aired. "Because I have much more to say to you, mister. Like how I would be stupid to give you another chance once you gave up on me."

"I agree. You would be stupid to give me another chance."

His easy concession only further incensed her. "Are you kidding me right now?"

"Spring, I came back for you. Because you're right. Okay? I know you can do better than me. I'm entitled and arrogant. I'm stubborn and I let my pride do most of the talking for me. I also seem to have a knack for getting into fights."

"All true," she spat.

"You're also right when you say I can't do any better." His head tilted to the left as he considered her. "But I want to be with you, Spring Astin. I want to be there with you when you wake up early in the morning and sing show tunes while you make pancakes. I want to be there for your mini meltdowns as well as those crazy, exhausting, and exuberant moments of excitement."

With each statement, Marshall took a step closer. Closer. Until he stood in front of her with barely inches to spare.

So close Spring craned her neck to stare up at his face. "You're really not painting an appealing picture of me, Professor."

"What I'm trying to say is that I've never been good with taking chances. Ever. I get stuck in what I think and what I feel and what I know, stuck in my comfort zone."

"Sounds boring," she said with a straight face.

"Very boring," he agreed. "When I met you, you were... well, you were everything *outside* of that little zone. Everything I was sure was not right for me."

"Now I suppose you've come to tell me that you've changed your mind?"

Could it be true?

"It's you. It's *always* been you." The statement was straightforward. Simple. "I've never had luck with any other relationships because I've been waiting to meet you. Now that I have, I'd be stupid to let you go. And I *never* want to let you go, Spring."

Pursing her lips, she broke eye contact, staring up at the sky. "Halloween is almost here. You were going to miss it."

"Are you even listening to me?"

"There's still time for you to make up for almost messing up my favorite holiday."

His face broke into a lazy smile. "Please. Tell me what you have in mind."

"Oh, I have quite a few things in mind. You are not getting off the hook that easily. In fact, I might never let you off the hook. I haven't decided yet."

"I deserve it." Marshall inclined his head meekly. "Keep me on the hook as long as you want. As long as you *keep me*."

"Not sure if I've made up my mind about that, either. But we can start to find out," Spring said at last. Then held out her hand. "Come on. There's still a little time left."

"Time for what?"

"For candy, silly. Candy, haunted houses, and kisses under the full moon. Time to find happily-ever-after."

Happily-ever-after...it didn't seem possible, and yet here he was, offering her that very thing if he was brave enough to admit it. And suddenly he knew he was brave enough. He wanted it all, all of those things and more, and it had taken him too long to admit it to himself. Too many nights of lying awake beating himself up over the decision to leave.

So...why leave? Why *not* take a chance on the love of his life?

He took Spring's hand without hesitation and allowed her to take the lead. Because he now knew that resistance was futile.

<hr>

The three matchmakers of Cinnamon Bay didn't need to spy. Or so Trixie told herself, leaning over the railing of the boardwalk and staring at the rapidly retreating figures of Spring and Marshall as they made their way laughing toward the surf.

A beach picnic. And the start of something wonderful.

"What did I tell you?" Trixie crowed. "I knew they would fall hard for each other. And it only took me a week. A week! You should be shaking in your loafers, ladies. I am the new record-holder."

"Liar!" Birdie scoffed. "It was *two and a half* weeks because he was more stubborn than you planned for. He almost left town. He made it to the airport before he finally came to his senses. And that's not even accounting for the scene they made during the boardwalk bash. I never want to step foot near that damn haunted house again."

"Either way, I see how you're trying to shift the focus away from my very obvious victory." Trixie placed a hand over her heart, gazing toward the sky. Sunlight glinted off her silvery curls. "Those two were made to complement each other. I'm glad they finally stopped fighting their feelings. Or at least I'm glad *he* stopped fighting *his* feelings. She recognized hers immediately. I knew she was the right woman for him."

"Maybe you'll get the uncle, you old crow," Hattie said with a hoot, nudging Birdie with her elbow.

Birdie turned her nose up. "I still think that I should have been the one to handle Spring." She pointedly ignored Hattie's obvious indication that she had a crush on the old fisherman. "After all, I took care of her best friend, Mecca. You stole this victory from me, Trixie, and I will not soon forget it."

Trixie blew her off with a burst of air through rounded lips. "Pfft. You'll get the next one. Stop complaining."

The three turned in unison away from the railing. With business at the coffee shop booming, there were still places to be, things to accomplish.

And matches to make.

THE END

Continue the Cinnamon Bay series and keep up with all the latest news

https://www.acinnamonbayromance.com/

For Author updates, sign up for Brea's newsletter
www.breaviragh.com/newsletter

ABOUT THE AUTHOR

BREA VIRAGH is a USA Today bestselling contemporary and paranormal romance writer based in the Blue Ridge Mountains. She is a proud Gryffindor, a graduate of Brakebills, and a member of Fairy Tail. Klaus Hargreeves is her bestie. When she isn't writing and daydreaming about her newest project, her hobbies include binge-watching HGTV, scouring thrift shops for goodies, and maintaining her alpha status among her puppy and three cats.

Read More from Brea Viragh

www.breaviragh.com

www.ingramcontent.com/pod-product-compliance
Lightning Source LLC
Chambersburg PA
CBHW071511150726
48000CB00002B/531